Choosing Nellie

by Anna Huckabee

cover design by germancreative;
artwork courtesy depositphotos.com

ISBN: 9781095528075

To my cousins

All 45 of you

The 44 who are still with me,

and the one who is already in heaven.

You helped make me the person I am today.

Thank you.

Chapter One

Boston, Massachusetts, Spring 1922

Nellie stared across the ballroom floor. Debutantes in white dresses floated across its surface in step with the waltz, clutching partners wearing black tuxedos. Nellie had never been a debutante. People from her small town in the middle of no-where Maine would consider it pretentious. She'd lost her chance to come out into society with other girls her age and that had given her a distinct disadvantage.

The strains of one waltz faded and the orchestra played the beginning notes of another. Partners across the floor rearranged themselves. No one seemed to notice Nellie standing on the fringes of the floor.

Two women conversed behind her. Their words filtered through the orchestral music filling the room.

"I heard she's been jilted twice. First time, it was some doctor from her backwoods hometown. The second was Edward Reid."

"She's the girl the Reids were talking about?" The woman sounded as horrified as if she'd heard Nellie concealed a tail under her dress or ate babies. Nellie cringed.

“Opal said the girl manipulated Edward into proposing. As soon as they found out, they made him break it off. Poor fellow carried around the stigma until he got married last fall.”

Nellie had heard about Edward’s quick marriage to a girl in another city a few months ago. Clearly, the gossips behind her had forgotten the scandal surrounding the wedding and the reason it had been a quiet affair. His parents had stayed out of society all winter. Someone had told Aunt Ida Edward’s wife had entered confinement until the birth of their baby.

The women weren’t finished.

“You know Opal and Edward Sr. No one was good enough for their boy,” said the first woman.

“Especially not some other man’s seconds.”

Nellie’s cheeks flamed with embarrassment. She wasn’t any man’s seconds. She wanted to whip around and tell those horrible women what really happened. But then she’d be admitting she was eavesdropping.

“I say her aunt needs to ship her back to whatever little village she came from. I wonder if she’s still here because they’re hoping to get her married off before she’s too old.”

“And saddle one of our society men with her history? They wouldn’t dare assume the possibility.”

“I know. In their place, I’m not sure I’d do much differently. She has more options here in Boston than she would wherever she’s from.”

“But how would a country bumpkin like her ever learn to function in our society? Look at her. Cheap clothes in last season’s style. Cheap jewelry. There’s no way she’d ever fit in here.”

Nellie stiffened and forced herself to not look down at her dress or touch her necklace. Her gloved fingers fidgeted with her dress involuntarily. She brought them up and clasped her hands in front of her. A hand at her elbow made her jump.

"What's this?" said Aunt Ida, who had appeared at her side. "Why so jumpy?"

Nellie shook her head and said nothing. She didn't trust her voice not to break.

"I don't want you to be a wallflower all evening. Your father and uncle have both agreed to dance with you. It's the only way you'll catch anyone's eye." Aunt Ida scanned the room, then waved her hand to attract the attention of the two men making their way around the perimeter of the ballroom floor.

"I'll never catch anyone's eye," Nellie muttered. "It's too late."

"Too late? Who said it was too late? You're twenty-three, not dead. Many girls have married when they were your age or older. Though, I do agree it only gets harder to find someone every passing year. It gets more difficult to compete with these pretty young things coming up."

Nellie glared at her aunt's back as the woman turned to greet her husband and brother. Nellie's father stepped close and offered his arm.

"May I have the next dance?" His eyes twinkled at Nellie.

She relaxed and gave him a small smile. "I'd enjoy that, Daddy."

As the strains of the next dance floated through the room, Daniel Greene led his daughter onto the ballroom floor.

"Why so sad?" he asked and they took the first tentative steps. A moment later they'd found their rhythm and whirled, as one, with the rest of the dancers.

"I thought coming to Boston would help me get away from all the gossips. It would give me a chance to live my life without having to constantly be reminded of things I've done in the past. Seems it doesn't work that way at all." Nellie heaved a huge sigh.

"What do you mean?"

"I overheard those two women over there talking about me. They knew all about what happened with Dr. Coburg in Walton. I guess I shouldn't be surprised when people know what happened with Edward last year."

"The situation Edward got himself into was unfortunate, but not your fault and you shouldn't bear the blame for it."

"Ah, but I am," Nellie said with a sad smile. "They said I tried to manipulate him to get my way."

Her father raised an eyebrow. Nellie flushed and turned away from his stern gaze. "You did manipulate. In both situations — the one with Dr. Coburg and your relationship with Edward."

Nellie's flush changed from one of embarrassment to one of anger. "So you agree with those old biddies who think I'm stuck an old maid because I've been jilted?"

"I didn't say that. This isn't the time or place to argue about it. I'm sorry you're still the recipient of their wagging tongues."

"I can't do anything to suit them. Even my dress and Grandma's necklace aren't good enough. They said I look and act cheap."

Sadness filled her father's eyes and he squeezed the hand he held in his own. The last strains of the song faded into the arched ceiling and they returned to stand beside her aunt and uncle.

The evening faded from one dance to another. Nellie danced with her father once more. It was the only other time she was asked. Finally, she'd had enough. Pleading a headache, she told her father she was going home. She went in search of her cloak, and had Uncle Charles' car sent around for her. The chauffeur drove her to her Uncle's house, dropped her at the front door of their townhome and returned to the party.

Once in the privacy of her room, Nellie shrugged out of her dress and pulled her nightgown over her head, leaving the dress in a heap on the floor. With shaking fingers, she pulled the pins out of her hair and shook out the curls. She didn't bother brushing out the tangles. Instead, she turned out the lights and threw herself onto her bed. The darkness gave her the privacy she desired.

How dare people be so cruel and unfeeling? How dare they make assumptions about her without ever learning the truth? How dare they sit there, all high and mighty, and make decisions about her without giving her a choice? Who were they to say if she'd marry or not?

All she wanted, all she'd ever wanted, was to marry a nice man. She preferred he was rich. Or maybe a doctor like her father. Dr. Coburg had been both. She'd met his family since coming to Boston. They were a snooty lot who looked down their noses at anyone not in their own social circle. She'd been thankful on more than one occasion they hadn't married. Oh, he'd married alright, and not that nurse trollop who stole him away from Nellie. No, he'd come back to Boston from his grand adventure in the backwoods and married the girl his family had chosen for him. They'd set him up with a practice on the outskirts of town and all the best clientele.

Nellie flopped onto her back and glared at the ceiling. The brilliant moon lit her room. She stared at the plaster scrollwork along the top of the wall. Her eyes followed the now familiar pattern.

They were all a pack of liars and hypocrites, saying one thing to your face and stabbing you in the back. Dr. Coburg's family had done it. So had Edward's.

Edward. Surely she wasn't to blame for what happened there? He'd been attentive, eager to spend time with her. Yes, she might have encouraged him more than was proper. She might have flirted with him. He was handsome. And rich. Even better, he was an up and coming banker whose father was backing Edward's branch in another city. Edward hadn't been in Boston very often during the last months of their relationship, which may have been part of the problem.

If only Edward could have gotten established in less time. If only her parents hadn't insisted they wait two years. If only they hadn't decided she needed to live with them in Hollis. She'd been happy in Boston. At least if she was there, she could see Edward when he came to visit. He never wanted to visit Hollis.

Whoever said "absence makes the heart grow fonder" was an idiot.

Absence hadn't made Edward's heart grow fonder. He'd forgotten all about Nellie, despite the fact she wrote him every day. He'd fallen into the arms of some other girl instead. Nellie had heard it was a shotgun wedding. A rush job. They had to get married before the scandal of the couple's actions ruined Edward's future hopes and dreams.

Aunt Ida said she'd been saved from a terrible fate. Men who wandered before marriage kept wandering afterward. Nellie hoped this harsh judgement wasn't true, despite how much he'd hurt her.

The front door opened, then closed. Nellie heard voices ascending the stairs. Aunt Ida's tinkling laughter, followed by Uncle Charles' deeper tones. At least someone had enjoyed the ball.

Her bedroom door opened and she could see her father's face through the crack, a shadow in the beam of light from the hall. Nellie froze and closed her eyes. She carefully controlled her breathing so he'd think she was already asleep.

The door closed again. Nellie opened her eyes and flopped onto her side to face the wall. She ran her fingertips over the velvety wallpaper. A tear slid down her cheek onto the pillowcase, followed by another, and another. Hot tears. Lonely tears.

It wasn't fair society got to decide which girls were eligible for marriage and which weren't. It wasn't fair all those debutantes would be engaged or married by the end of the year, while she'd be passed over yet again. She didn't even know anyone she'd like to marry. At this point she'd probably have to settle for some rich widower with children. She didn't even like children, though she suspected and even hoped she'd like them more if they were her own.

Nellie balled her hand into a fist and hit her pillow. She hit it again and again as the tears streamed faster down her face. She wished she could scream. It hurt to hold it inside. But young ladies didn't scream. They carried themselves with proper decorum at all times, even in bed at night when no one could see them.

She buried her face in her pillow and let the sobs wrack her body. Her mother would say she was being dramatic and overreacting. Maybe she was. Her mother wasn't here to stop her now, was she? Her mother was more concerned with packing up Grandma's house and selling it than she was taking care of her only daughter. Aunt Ida had been there for her when she needed it. Still, not even Aunt Ida would let her behave in an unladylike manner.

Nellie's sobs calmed and she felt herself relax and drift to sleep. She fought it with everything in her. She wanted to lay here, awake and miserable all night. She hadn't counted on the riot of emotions draining her. She rolled onto her side again and tried to dredge up the emotions she'd been feeling only moments before. Nothing worked. Nellie fell asleep, despite her best efforts to stay awake.

Chapter Two

"Excuse me, Mr. Burke."

Warren fanned the cards in his hand and heaved a sigh before he turned to look at the footman standing behind his right shoulder.

"Your Aunt is on the telephone. She requests your immediate attention. She said it was an emergency."

Warren returned his gaze to the cards in his hand. It was a terrible hand. He stacked them and dropped them on the table in front of him. "I'm out. If you'll excuse me gentlemen."

A murmur traveled around the table. A couple of the other men groaned. One leaned back in his chair with a smug grin.

Warren followed the footman through the maze of tables in the gaming room. They entered a private office with a desk, on which sat a telephone with the earpiece propped to one side. A woman's angry cries wafted through it. Warren lifted the earpiece but waited until the cries died down before placing it against his ear. He brought the mouthpiece up and spoke into it.

"Aunt Lou," he said, carefully keeping his tone even and light, "how can I help you this evening?"

"I told you not to go to that idiotic ball. My maid has gone for the night and little Sophia has vomited all over the new carpet in my drawing room. You must come help me rouse people to get this cleaned up. No one is answering my bell."

The woman was almost screaming. Warren took a deep breath and let it out through his nose before he said anything. "Did you overfeed the dog again, Aunt? You know the veterinarian said not to give her any desserts no matter how she begs."

Silence hung in the air, ominous after all the screaming. Warren waited. He could feel the heat of his aunt's anger through the phone.

"Are you saying this is my fault?" The old woman's tone was calm but cutting.

"Did you feed the dog any of your dessert at dinner?"

"Of course I did. She eats everything I eat."

"Then yes, I'm saying this is your fault."

The silence fairly crackled with her rage. Warren waited long moments before speaking again.

"I will, however, see what I can do about rousing someone to clean it. Give me a few minutes to get my hat and coat, then I'll be right over."

Warren replaced the earpiece in its cradle, disconnecting the call. He rested his hands on the desktop and leaned onto it. His aunt needed more care than he could give her. The crotchety old woman had driven away every maid she'd had in the last ten years. Warren struggled to keep staff around longer than a few weeks, three or four months at most. The exception was her old butler. But he and his wife no longer lived on the premises. The only way he'd been able to keep the cleaning lady was to pay her son's way through school. That poor woman bore more abuse than anyone.

Warren straightened and made his way through the ballroom to retrieve his coat. He had no interest in the debutante ball. He'd only come for a rousing card game with men he only saw once or twice a year. His business required he crisscross the country and spend weeks away. He had no time for social interaction when he was in Boston.

He found his car and drove to his aunt's house, stopping at the cleaning lady's on his way. The saintly woman grudgingly agreed to come clean the mess for a few extra dollars and an extra day off later in the month. Warren couldn't remember how many days she got off already, but he was confident she would remind him.

Aunt Louellen paced the floor, anger seething out of every pore. She held her Boston terrier in the crook of one arm, and a cane draped over the other. Warren knew she wanted to give him an earful but would hold her tongue until the cleaning lady was gone. He had an earful he wanted to give her, too. They glared at each other while the cleaning lady scrubbed up the mess. He paid her for her work, gave her cab fare, and sent her home.

Aunt Louellen started talking the moment the door closed behind the cleaning woman and her footsteps had faded. "I've told you again and again I cannot manage on my own here every night. Something always happens. I've been abandoned by everyone who ever cared about me, including you. You spend as little time here as possible. If you don't find a way to remedy the problem, I'll bequeath my estate to someone else."

"Don't hold your money over me like the sword of Damocles. I don't need your money, Aunt. You can do with it whatever you choose."

"But what else do I have left?" The old lady's tone changed. It was plaintive, bordering on a whine. "Everyone I loved is gone. I've been left on my own. I have no one."

"For one thing, you could be kinder to those who are making an effort to take care of you. Like the lovely cleaning lady who came out in the middle of the night. Or your cook who slaves away to feed your fragile digestion, only to have you feed half of it to a dog who's going to vomit it back up on the new carpet."

Warren realized he was still holding his hat. He tossed it onto a side table and threw his cloak over a chair. Then he faced his aunt again.

Aunt Louellen absently stroked the dogs head while huge tears rolled down her cheeks. Warren narrowed his eyes. She was trying to manipulate him again. It wouldn't work.

"The dog is all I have left. I should leave my estate to the dog." Aunt Louellen's voice caught on the last words.

"If that's what you want. I'll contact the lawyer tomorrow and have him draw up the papers."

"Insufferable man!" Aunt Louellen stomped her foot, her tears replaced by anger. "How can you be so cold and unfeeling?" She was screaming again. The dog trembled in her arms.

"Because you are cold and unfeeling, Aunt. You care nothing for the feelings of those around you. You chase away everyone I hire to help you because of your capricious emotions, your pride, your insistence on having your way."

She sniffed. "It's my house. Why shouldn't things be done my way?"

"And then I have to go get the cleaning lady in the middle of the night because you wouldn't listen to the veterinarian and not feed your dog rich food."

Aunt Louellen whirled away and stalked up the hall. "I'm going to bed. I should have done so hours ago. I assume you are leaving again in the morning?"

Warren lifted his gaze to the ceiling. He clenched and unclenched his fists. He had to keep his temper. His tone was even when he finally spoke.

"I'll be in Boston for a few days this time. I hope my coming and going doesn't disturb you. I'll try to stay out of your way as much as possible."

"No matter. I'll inform the cook to fix food for you as well. Good night." The old woman disappeared into a doorway up the hall and shut it behind her with a little more force than necessary.

Warren's jaw clenched so tight it hurt. He clomped up the stairs to the bedroom he used when he was in Boston. He owned a house, but had rented it because he never stayed long enough to justify hiring his own staff.

Maybe he should shorten his stay. Was there any way to accomplish everything in three or four days instead of a week? He rubbed his hands over his face and considered. No, he had appointments every day.

He groaned as he shrugged out of his evening jacket and tossed it across the back of a chair. He sank onto the chair to remove his shoes.

He had to do something about Aunt Lou. She was correct about many things, first of which was the fact she needed someone with her all the time. The octogenarian's tongue was no less sharp than it had been forty years ago. Not that Warren had been around then. His parents had told him stories about his father's eccentric sister. She had become so cantankerous in recent years no one wanted to be around her. It didn't help most of those from her generation had either passed away or lost their independence because of their age. The fact she got around as well as she did was probably more a testament to her stubbornness than anything else.

Warren settled in bed, a bedside lamp providing light for him to read until he had calmed enough to be able to fall asleep. He opened the book to the marker he'd left in it the previous evening. But he couldn't focus on the words enough to comprehend them. After reading the same paragraph three times, he was still unable to remember what it said. He closed the book and returned it to the table. Then he turned off the lamp and slid down to settle into his pillows.

What could he do about Aunt Lou? No one he hired stayed around long. None of her friends bothered to put forth an effort to visit.

And why not? She was hateful and cutting and demanding and hurtful. Years of practice had honed her skill. Warren remembered, as a child, he'd been afraid of her and what she might say to him.

Where could he even begin searching for a companion for his aunt? She'd injure anyone he hired and they wouldn't last.

Warren pushed himself up to sit and turned the lamp back on. He found the small notebook and pencil he kept next to the bed. He'd need someone much younger than his aunt, a young woman, preferably unmarried so she'd be free to live with Aunt Lou most of the time. He wrote the thoughts down as fast as they came. She'd need to be stubborn and sharp witted in order to outlast the onslaught she was sure to meet on a daily basis. She'd need to be from similar social status as his aunt. He secretly suspected that was why the people he hired didn't last. She gave them little to no respect and no thanks whatsoever for their hard work.

Warren tapped the pencil against the list. Could he put an advertisement in the paper? He feared it would attract the wrong sort of girl, someone searching for a job, not simply desiring to offer companionship to an old woman. Maybe he could ask as he fulfilled his appointments over the course of this next week. His doctor and business associates would be more likely to know the kind of young woman he hoped to find and be better equipped to help him find her.

His thoughts settled, Warren replaced the notebook and pencil on the table and turned off the lamp once more. He laid down, suddenly drowsy and closed his eyes. He felt as though a weight had lifted, at least until tomorrow when he actually began his search for a companion for his aunt.

Chapter Three

"You appear to be healthy as a horse. As usual." Dr. Greene dropped the stethoscope around his neck and faced his patient.

"My dad was my age when his health started its decline. I'd rather be safe than sorry. With modern medical advances, there is no reason I should suffer as he did." Warren buttoned his shirt and reached for his waistcoat.

"Your father made other life choices from an early age that contributed to his overall lack of good health. For one thing, it's clear you stay far more active than he ever did."

Warren shrugged. "Again, better safe than sorry. I travel for business. It's easier to travel when you're in good health than in poor."

"It's easier to do anything when you're in good health."

Warren chuckled. It felt good to laugh. "True."

"Anything else I can help you with before you go?"

Warren thought about the list in his coat pocket. He'd planned to ask his associates. This was proving more difficult than he'd imagined. He'd said nothing at his first appointment of the morning. Here he was, at his doctor's appointment, setting himself up to say nothing again. He steeled himself against the sudden nerves and pulled out the list. Dr. Greene knew his aunt. Both he and his father had treated her for her whole life.

“As you well know, my Aunt Louellen is getting up in years,” he began. “She needs someone to stay with her full time, to look after her in case of accidents. Frankly, she needs companionship. All this time by herself is making her more disagreeable than she was before. Would you happen to know of any young women who’d be willing to be a companion for a grumpy old woman?”

Dr. Greene glanced over the hastily scrawled note Warren handed him. “She’s a tough old thing. Stubborn. Honestly, she’s in better health than women half her age. She could live for decades longer.”

“I’m aware of this. I’m also aware I’d be asking this young woman to give up all chance at a social life. I know most young women would never consider it.”

“Do you think your aunt would tolerate a young widow living with her?”

“Do you know of any young widows without children? Or even older widows, for that matter? My aunt hates children. She hates discussing children and what they do. Anyone who stayed with her would have to refrain from this topic of conversation altogether.”

“I see.” Dr. Greene tapped his lip with his finger and stared at the list. “I can think of one option, actually. This opportunity might be a godsend for her. I don’t know how she would receive it. Are you free to luncheon with my family today? You could present it to her yourself.”

Warren raised an eyebrow in question as he shrugged into his jacket.

The doctor continued. "My daughter needs something to occupy her time. Her interactions with society have not been positive. She has no attachments and is encumbered by nothing. I feel she would make a good companion for your aunt, if she chooses to do so. She certainly fits the requirements listed here."

"I have a lunch engagement, but I'm free for tea this afternoon."

"That will work. We are staying with my sister and her husband while in Boston. I'll notify my sister you are coming and make sure my daughter is present for tea."

"Until this afternoon." Warren shook his doctor's hand. He felt lighter at the prospect of having found someone with so little difficulty. He only hoped the lady in question would agree to stay with his aunt.

∞

Nellie woke slowly to sunlight pouring in her window and streaming across her bed. She stretched. She didn't feel like being awake yet, but since her curtains were open to the daylight, she'd probably be unable to go back to sleep.

A tap on the door was followed by Aunt Ida's head appearing through the opening. "Look who's finally awake. Good morning sleepyhead."

Puzzled, Nellie glanced at the alarm clock next to her bed. Ten-thirty in the morning. She'd slept longer than it felt. "I must have been tired after the ball last night."

"I don't see how. You barely danced."

Nellie frowned at her aunt, who'd felt it necessary to remind Nellie why she'd left early.

"Not that it matters," said Aunt Ida with a dismissive wave of her hand. "Your father rang. He's bringing a guest for tea this afternoon. A certain Warren Burke. He wants to meet you." Aunt Ida was beaming.

Nellie pushed herself up in bed and tried to smooth her tangled hair.

"He's one of the richest, most eligible bachelors in town," Aunt Ida continued. "Your father said he had an offer for you."

Nellie's eyes widened. "What kind of offer?"

"I don't know. I think it could only mean one thing!" Aunt Ida clasped her hands in front of her and squealed like a little girl. "Everything will have to be well chaperoned, of course. But we'll make every effort for you to get to know him."

Nellie swung her legs over the side of the bed and slid her feet into her house shoes. She wrapped a dressing gown over her nightgown, then shuffled across the room. She grabbed her brush off the dressing table. Uncertainty filled her chest and stomach with nervous flutters. Her hand shook as she dragged her brush through the matted tangles in her hair.

"I don't know," she said after several minutes. "How could he want to get to know me, maybe marry me, if we've never even met. I'm certain I would have remembered the most eligible bachelor in Boston."

"He's no where near your age," said Aunt Ida. "He's only tolerably handsome, too. But one can put up with tolerable looks in a man, as long as they are accompanied by enough money. I assure you, this is the case with Warren Burke."

Nellie winced as the brush snagged in her hair. "I want to believe you, but I'm afraid to get my hopes up. I can't handle any more dashed hopes right now." She stared at her reflection in the mirror, taking in the still puffy eyes and red nose from her angry tears the previous night.

"Don't worry about a thing, my dear. He'll love you. We have to make sure everything is done right and proper. Now, put on your prettiest dress and come down for some coffee. We'll go over what the cook is planning for tea and see if anything needs to be changed."

Nellie gave her aunt a weak smile and returned to brushing her hair. Once the tangles had been smoothed out, a few twists and pins had it up and neat on the back of her head. She pulled an everyday dress out of the wardrobe and put it on. She knew Aunt Ida would send her up to change before their company arrived, but she didn't feel like being stiff and proper all day. She washed her face and cleaned her teeth. A final glance in the mirror showed her eyes were less puffy and she had a normal colored nose. Nellie slipped her shoes on and hurried downstairs.

Aunt Ida frowned when she saw Nellie. "You'll have to change before he comes," she said.

Nellie sipped the hot coffee her aunt had prepared. She dreaded the long, boring day stretching before her. She skimmed the newspaper headlines and then disappeared into the library with a book. The words on the page blurred in and out around her doubt-filled thoughts.

What if her father had set up the whole thing to marry her off?

What if Warren Burke got to know her and took off, like Dr. Coburg and Edward?

What if she hated him, but he was the last man to ever ask her to marry him?

Nellie couldn't handle these doubts. She dropped the book onto a side table, then hurried upstairs in search of her hat and coat.

Aunt Ida caught her as she headed out the front door. "Where are you going?" She sounded panicked.

"I'll be in the park, if you want me."

"Make sure you're back in time for tea."

"Tea is hours away. I'll be back long before then." Nellie pulled the door closed behind her.

The spring sunshine had warmed the air enough so it wasn't cold, but Nellie still appreciated her coat. She walked to the tiny community park at the end of the block, then navigated the short trail through the flowerbeds. A few of the flowers were making a valiant effort to remind everyone of the season. Yellow crocuses carpeted one bed, interspersed with purple hyacinths. Their fragrance wafted on the light breeze. Nellie sucked in the heavenly scent, then shivered as the cool breeze chilled her. She pulled her coat tighter. Farther up the path, apple and cherry trees were budding. In another week they'd be able to smell those flowers on the breeze all the way at her aunt's house.

Gran would have loved this. Gran had hated winter — the cold, the endless snow, the early evening darkness. Her favorite season had always been spring. She'd planted bulbs for flowers sure to bloom the minute it was warm enough. Gran always planted her garden too early and had to replant it at least once.

Gran sat on the back steps and soaked in the sunshine as soon as the snow melted.

Nellie had traveled the path around the park twice already. She started around it a third time and lifted her face to the warmth of the early afternoon sunshine.

Oh, how she wished she'd treated Gran better in those last months before she'd come to live in Boston. Shame filled her as she thought of the things she'd said, the accusations she'd leveled against one of the kindest women God had put on the earth. Nellie didn't think the pain and regret she felt from her poor choices would ever fade. She dreaded what people would think if they ever found out. They already thought so poorly of her.

If this Warren Burke fellow ever found out, would he still be interested? If he was, indeed, interested in a relationship anyway.

Nellie gave herself a mental shake. She'd come out in the sunshine to help herself feel better. To make herself stop thinking all these dark, doubt-filled thoughts. Here she was, no better than when she'd left. She started another trip around the park.

What if, to make amends for everything she'd done, she started helping out at the children's hospital? Her father had been after her to get out of the house and give back to the community. She didn't like children, but she could tolerate them for a few hours a week.

There was also the ladies aid society at church. Nellie thought they put together barrels of clothing and blankets for missionaries around the world. She could always help there if the hospital didn't work out. In fact, maybe that was a better idea. There would be no children involved at all.

Nellie's spirits began to rise. She simply needed to get out of the house and do something productive. Everyone had been encouraging her to do it. Those old gossips last night probably never did anything worthwhile. She'd show them.

With lighter steps, she left the park and returned to her aunt's and uncle's house. By the time she'd bounded up the front steps and burst into the hall, she'd forgotten all about her sour mood.

Chapter Four

"Mr. Burke! It's so good to see you again. It's been too long."

Ida Hayes offered her hand to Warren. He shook it. "Thank you for the invitation, Mrs. Hayes."

The lady led the way into a drawing room and indicated a chair. Warren waited until she'd seated herself before sitting down. "My husband phoned to inform me he wouldn't be home from the office in time for tea. But my brother and niece are somewhere in the house. My footman is fetching them. In the meantime, how do you take your tea?"

Warren shifted in his chair, already uncomfortable. He clenched his jaw and forced a smile. He was desperate for someone to stay with his aunt. He could endure mindless chitchat in pursuit of his goal.

"I prefer it black," he said.

"No cream or sugar?" The lady sounded surprised.

"Black is fine." He took the cup she offered him and set it on a side table to let it cool.

The door opened and Dr. Greene entered, followed by a young woman. She was a pretty sort of thing, with light hair and blue eyes. She met his gaze boldly, like all young women these days. Yet, there was strength in her eyes. He could tell she wasn't one to back down easily. He was drawn to the fearlessness he saw in her. At least she didn't have one of those infernal bobs so popular right now and her dress wasn't too short. His aunt might tolerate a girl with a bob, but she'd never allow any calves showing. With this initial scrutiny, his mind was made up. He'd offer her the job.

"Mr. Burke," said Dr. Greene by way of greeting. "I'm glad you made it."

"Allow me to introduce my niece, Nellie, er, Eleanor," said Mrs. Hayes.

Warren met the frank gaze of the young woman, Eleanor. If he was honest, she looked more like a Nellie, but, again, his aunt would never call her by a nickname. If she took the job, she'd have to get used to her full name.

The ladies took their seats and Ida Hayes handed around tea, cakes, and inane conversation. Warren barely heard what she said. He didn't tolerate prattle and tended to tune it out. In that way, he was a lot like his aunt. He had no idea how to turn the topic around to the reason for his visit. Dr. Greene came to his rescue the moment he had finished his last bite of cake and set his empty plate on the side table.

"Warren had an unusual question for me when he stopped by my office earlier today. I thought he should pose the question to you ladies as well. Especially you, Nellie."

Ida Hayes leaned forward. An eager smile covered her face. Her gaze fluttered between himself and Nellie.

Nellie, on the other hand, had plastered a strained smile on her face, as if she was trying to be polite for her aunt's sake. Her hand rested on her stomach. She stared at him with a mixture of uncertainty and excitement.

What did they think he was going to ask? Had Greene told them nothing?

"My elderly aunt has been requesting I find her a companion. She lives alone. None of our help stays the night anymore. There have been incidents in the last few weeks requiring me to fetch someone after hours. Besides, she's lonely and, I think…I hope, would enjoy the company. Your father suggested you might be interested in this opportunity, Eleanor."

"Well." Ida Hayes exploded at the end of his speech. She glared at Warren and stood to her feet. "If you'll excuse me, I'll call someone to clear away our tea things." Then she swept from the room.

Warren turned to Dr. Greene for assistance, but that man looked as confused as Warren felt.

Nellie's mouth was pressed in a straight line, lower lip quivering, her hand still clutched at her stomach. "Thank you for your kind offer." Her voice shook with the words. "If it's possible, could you give me a few days to consider? I'll let you know as soon as I've made a decision."

Warren's confusion changed into panic - a panic he hadn't felt all day because he'd thought this was a sure thing. She'd accept his offer and they could begin steps of introducing her to his aunt and moving her into the other bedroom in the townhome.

"I understand this is an unusual request, but I leave on a business trip in six days. I'll need to know as soon as possible so I can make other arrangements if you choose not to stay with her."

"Then I will try to make my decision by tomorrow. Good afternoon, Mr. Burke." Nellie stood and followed her aunt from the room.

Warren stared at the wall in front of him without seeing it. "Did you give them any indication as to the nature of my visit?"

"I didn't have the chance. I only arrived home from the office in time for tea and neither of the ladies were around." Dr. Greene clapped a hand on Warren's shoulder. "Have no fear, Burke. I'll bring Nellie around to it. You won't need to go in search of anyone else."

"Let's say you can't talk her into it. What then? Do I hire a live-in nurse? My aunt isn't ill. She's lonely"

"Maybe you could hire her ladies maid to stay overnight most of the week?"

Warren shook his head. "I only convinced her maid not to quit by promising she'd never have to stay overnight again." He noted his friend's puzzled expression. "My aunt can be…difficult. She dislikes most people. In fact, most of those she truly liked have passed. She lives in self-imposed isolation."

"I can't have my daughter living in a situation where your aunt will mistreat her."

"Have no fear of that, sir. My aunt has a sharp tongue and your daughter will need a thick skin to withstand the lashings she'll receive from it. But my aunt will not mistreat her. She's becoming aware of the fact that her words have driven everyone away. They will be in for an adjustment. My aunt is quite particular about how things should be done and she won't stand for nonsense. She despises the latest fashions and isn't afraid to tell anyone what she thinks. Your daughter appears to be conservative. They may not get on, but at least my aunt won't berate her for her clothing choices. She will need a backbone to stand up to my aunt."

"I can assure you Nellie has a backbone. I'm still not confident I've made a wise suggestion to my daughter." Dr. Greene shook his head. Warren noted the worry in his eyes.

"I give you every assurance she will be well."

"I'll hold you to it."

Warren bid Dr. Greene a good day and left for his aunt's house. He had infused more confidence into his words than he felt. He considered the repercussions of his words if his aunt took a disliking to the girl. The car bounced over the paving stones but Warren barely noticed. He was hoping he hadn't made promises, given assurances, outside his power to keep.

Chapter Five

Conversation around the dinner table was strained. Nellie wasn't hungry, but she forced herself to take bites of the food so her father wouldn't worry. He always seemed to notice how much or little she ate.

Aunt Ida asked Uncle Charles how work had gone for him. He responded in typical Uncle Charles fashion - short answers that revealed very little. When she saw she would get nothing else from her husband, she turned to her brother.

"How was your day at the office, Daniel?"

"It was fine. Interesting. Not too busy." He gave his sister a strained smile.

"No unusual ailments or unique patients?"

"No, nothing out of the ordinary."

"You can't say that, Daniel. You brought one of your unique patients to our house for tea."

"Burke is a family friend, not a unique patient. I brought him as a favor. You've been acting strangely ever since his visit and I can't figure out why."

"You didn't think to at least mention the reason he was coming when you called to inform me?"

"I didn't have time. Besides, it was his news to deliver and I'd say he did his job just fine. You women, on the other hand. I don't know what to think about you all. Why did you think he was coming to tea?"

"You said he had an offer for Nellie."

"He did have an offer for Nellie. Nellie sits home all day, every day. It isn't healthy. She needs to get out more, meet new people."

"And this is your solution to the problem? She goes to live with an old woman who hates everyone."

"Ida, you don't need to be cruel. Loneliness drives people to push everyone away, exacerbating the loneliness."

"You are impossible, Daniel."

Daniel placed his fork next to his plate, folded his arms across his chest and leaned toward his sister, seated across from him at the table. Now he was angry, an unusual emotion for him to display. "Impossible how? Because I care about my only child and desire she get out and enjoy life? What kind of offer did you think he was going to make?"

Ida pushed the food around her plate and wouldn't meet her brother's intense gaze. "I thought he might be coming to call on her."

"Why would I allow him to call on my daughter when he's never met her?"

"How else would they get to know one another if he didn't call on her?"

Daniel barked a laugh. "You think this successful businessman is desperate enough to desire marriage with a woman he's never met? I assure you, he already knows dozens of eligible women."

"He would want someone from his own social circle, not some random business associate's daughter."

"There are many young women in his social circle, Ida, and Nellie isn't one of them."

Ida stiffened. Her expression darkened. "Are you saying Nellie isn't good enough for him? Your own daughter!"

"I said nothing of the sort. I said we aren't in his social circle. Nellie had never met him before today. The only reason I know him is because I'm his doctor, as was Father. You see, your assumption did more harm than good."

"At least *I* assume Nellie has a chance at marriage with a rich businessman like Warren Burke!"

Daniel rubbed his face with his hand. "Nellie has a chance at marriage with anyone she chooses to marry," he said wearily. "But I prefer she know the person longer than an afternoon before she make such a decision."

Nellie's eyes met her father's. She knew he was thinking about the two failed relationships she'd had. Shame filled her. She had decided the moment she met both men she would do whatever it took to marry them. It had not turned out well. She dropped her gaze to her plate.

"Warren is worried about his aunt living alone. He said she has been in situations when she needed someone, and no one was there. He doesn't want that to happen when he's on the other side of the globe."

Aunt Ida sniffed. "This is the same woman who fired her newly hired ladies maid because she came in wearing a dress that showed her ankles."

Nellie's wide eyes flew to her aunt's.

"That's not all," Aunt Ida continued. "She refused to allow the butler who had been with their family for decades to continue to live in her house because she insisted his wife was stealing their antique silver. Nothing was ever proved, of course. I'm amazed the man still works for her after the false accusations she's leveled against his wife."

"I'm sure Nellie will be fine. Burke seems to think so. You can't believe everything you hear, Ida. I doubt Warren Burke would continue to employ a thief."

"Nellie doesn't need to be shut up in a house with an old woman all day. She needs to get out, experience life."

"She needs a vision bigger than the desperation of making sure she doesn't end up an old maid."

"She could go into nursing or teaching. Anything is better than what you are asking of her, Daniel."

"I'm sitting right here!" Nellie cried into the midst of their argument.

Both siblings looked at her. Her father heaved a huge sigh. Aunt Ida returned her attention to the food on her plate. She dropped her fork onto it with a clatter and pushed it away.

"Have you given it any thought?" Her father asked, his tone more gentle. "I don't want to push you into anything you would dislike, but your aunt is correct, you need to get out more."

"You both know I'd hate nursing or teaching." Nellie shuddered involuntarily remembering the weeks in the children's ward of the hospital in Walton. "Yes, I'm thinking about it."

"Good," said her father. "What if I made arrangements with Mr. Burke for you to meet his aunt and see if you two could even get on? No sense moving you over there only to have her decide she hates you."

The idea brought Nellie a huge amount of relief. She hadn't had much success getting along with old women, either. And Mr. Burke's aunt sounded difficult. "I'd like that."

"I'll ring him after dinner," said her father. "Maybe we can visit her tomorrow."

Chapter Six

The following morning, they pulled to a stop in front of a brick townhouse not dissimilar to her aunt's and uncle's. Nellie and her father walked up the short path to the front stairs. A butler opened the door for them before they even knocked and showed them into a formal parlor. Nellie checked her shoes before walking across the white carpet. She was afraid to sit on any of the white velvet covered chairs.

Long minutes passed as they waited. Thirty minutes had gone by before a flustered butler returned to see if they wanted coffee. Her father declined for both of them. Another ten minutes passed before Mr. Burke entered the house and stepped into the parlor.

"Has my aunt been to see you yet?" he asked.

"I'm afraid not," Daniel said. "I have an appointment scheduled in a few minutes. Even if I leave now I'll be late. Maybe we could come again tomorrow?"

Mr. Burke scowled and turned on his heel. "Please, wait for a minute or two longer. I'll find out what has happened and inform you immediately."

Nellie heard his steps fade up the hall. She turned to her father. "Was this his idea or his aunt's?"

"He led me to believe it was his aunt's, though now I think about our conversation yesterday, he could have meant the idea was his. I didn't clarify."

They fell silent when they heard Mr. Burke's steps returning. A moment later he appeared in the doorway.

"She insists she has a headache and won't see you, which is utter nonsense. Dr. Greene, feel free to leave for your appointment. I'll personally make sure your daughter gets home safely."

Daniel turned to Nellie. "Is this alright with you?"

"I think so." If Nellie was honest, she was so nervous she felt sick. Why didn't this old lady want to see her? But then she'd have to go back and listen to Aunt Ida's gloating about how she'd been right the whole time. She lifted her chin. "You go on. I want to meet her."

Daniel pecked a kiss on his daughter's cheek. "Thanks, Burke. I look forward to hearing how it goes." He hurried from the room. Nellie saw him put on his hat as his brisk stride carried him up the short front walk and he entered their car.

"Shall we go introduce you to my aunt, Miss Greene? Her name is Louellen McGowen. She's eighty-four and today she insists she is bedridden. It will probably make her angry when I bring you to her room. Don't take anything she says to heart. Her cutting tongue is well known."

"I've heard stories," Nellie said.

"Good." Mr. Burke gave her a grim smile. "Shall we go?"

Mr. Burke motioned toward the hallway and Nellie fell into step behind him. She almost ran into his back when he stopped, suddenly, outside a closed door. "One more thing. You will go by Eleanor in this house for two reasons. First, my aunt hates monikers. She refuses to use them. Second, she will use any means to make you angry, including mocking your name.

Anything to justify dismissing you. Eleanor was the name of her best friend in her youth. The lady died giving birth to her first child. She will never mock your full name."

Nellie swallowed hard. What was she getting herself into?

"Are you ready?"

"As ready as I'll ever be."

Mr. Burke pushed open the door and entered the room. Nellie followed.

"Aunt Lou, this is Eleanor Greene. She's Dr. Greene's daughter. She stopped by today to meet you."

"I told you I didn't want any guests today. I have a headache." The old woman sniffed and pulled her dressing gown closer around her neck.

"And why wouldn't your head hurt when you have the curtains drawn on such a beautiful morning?" Mr. Burke stepped to the window and whisked open the curtains.

Sunlight streamed across the frail old woman in the bed. A tiny terrier nestled against her, waiting for the old woman to hand it morsels of food off the tray sitting to the side. It looked like the woman hadn't touched a bite of food, but had been feeding it to the dog. Mr. Burke glared at the scene before him, then a wicked grin parted his lips.

"The fresh air will do you good. It should ease your headache, make you better able to eat the delicious breakfast Cook made for you this morning." He turned back to the window and threw open the sash.

Both Nellie and the old lady gasped at his action.

"Close that window immediately!" the old lady cried. "Do you want Sophia to catch her death?"

"You can't spend your days in darkness. It isn't healthy. I'm leaving the window. If you want it closed, you'll have to get out of bed and do it yourself." Mr. Burke walked across the room to stand by the bed.

"Why did you bring her here today?" Louellen McGowen indicated Nellie without looking at her.

"I wanted the two of you to meet. I spoke with Dr. Greene about you yesterday. I told him you were lonely and I was worried about you while I'm away on business. I told him I thought you should have a companion and he said his daughter was available."

Louellen McGowen looked at Nellie for the first time. Her narrow eyes moved from the top of Nellie's head down to her shoes and back. Nellie had no doubt the woman saw every detail of her person.

"Why isn't she married already? A girl her age should be married and have children. What's wrong with her? It's not my job to entertain an old maid."

Nellie's eyes widened and jerked to Mr. Burke. How dare she? He gave a small, sharp jerk of his head. She bit her tongue.

"Aunt, you won't be entertaining her. She'll be here to provide companionship for you while I'm away."

"Because you are always so present and companionable when you *are* in town."

"I'm going to ignore that statement."

"I do not want or need another person in this house to make sure I behave myself." The old lady shifted her body away from them in the bed. The food tray rocked precariously. Nellie took a step forward to grab it but Mr. Burke waved her away.

"You told me the other night you did. So I'm taking steps to provide companionship for you, whether you want it or not. If it isn't Miss Greene, then it will be a live-in nurse. Because clearly you are too much of an invalid to be left alone." He turned to Nellie. "Thank you for coming Miss Greene. I'll see you to the door."

Nellie's eyebrows shot up but Mr. Burke motioned for her to stay silent and leave the room.

The old woman's plaintive voice followed them into the hall. "I don't want a live-in nurse. Bring the girl back. I'll have another look at her."

They filed back into the room and Nellie was once more subjected to Mrs. McGowen's scrutiny.

"How old are you, girl?" the old lady asked.

"Twenty-three." Nellie lifted her chin as she answered.

"What's wrong with you? Why aren't you married?"

"Nothing is wrong with me. I've had offers. None of them were right for me. Besides, who says a woman's only option is to marry and have babies?"

"I say, that's who!" cried Mrs. McGowen. The dog jumped at her cry, nearly upsetting the food tray once more. "Are you one of those intolerable suffragettes who demand equal rights for women? I won't have any of that in my house."

Mr. Burke narrowed his eyes at his aunt, but Nellie refused to back down. Her own words held an edge when she replied. "I'm not a suffragette. But I'm not going to sit around a house waiting for a man to come rescue me. Besides, I don't even like babies!"

The old woman sniffed and stroked her dog. "I never liked babies, either. I was so thankful I never had any of them when I was married. Though I suppose if I had we wouldn't be having this conversation."

She shifted until she could see her nephew. "Fine. I'll give Miss Greene a try for a few days and see if we can get along. I doubt this will work out. But I suppose she is better than a live-in nurse."

"She's better than sitting around all day with only a dog for company." said Mr. Burke. He leaned over and pecked his aunt's cheek. "I'll make arrangements with her father to bring her things over here and get her situated in the guest room. You must try to let this work."

"I'm not making any promises." Louellen McGowen fed another bit of food to the dog.

Mr. Burke led Nellie out of his aunt's room and back to the parlor. While they waited for the butler to bring her coat and hat, he finalized details.

"If it works for you, I'll send the car around tomorrow to retrieve you and your things and bring them here. We best not wait too long. Tonight would be better, but I imagine you can't be ready by then. Can you?" The last was said hopefully.

Nellie shook her head. "I don't think so."

His face fell. "Then tomorrow it is. Expect her to be difficult the first few days. She was up and dressed this morning early. But she went back to bed when I told her you were coming. It's how she is. You'll have to be firm. Don't be afraid to push back, just like you did a few minutes ago. It's good for her to have her opinions challenged. I'll be around for the first few days if anything goes wrong."

"I'm sure we'll be fine." Nellie smiled at him with more confidence than she felt.

The car arrived in front of the house. Mr. Burke went with her and held open the car door while she got inside. He gave the driver her address. "Until tomorrow, then," he said.

The car pulled away from the curb and started toward home. Nellie wondered what on earth she'd gotten herself into.

Chapter Seven

Ruffled lace curtains fluttered in the spring breeze coming from the open window. Matching lace hung over the canopy bed covered in a lace duvet. Nellie stepped carefully across the deep rose rug and peeked through the curtains. Mrs. McGowen's guest room was the prettiest room Nellie had ever seen.

Nellie watched while Mrs. McGowen's lady's maid unpacked the few items of clothing she'd brought with her. The woman stored the empty suitcase in the closet and returned downstairs while Nellie continued to stare out the window. People needed to think about the view when they placed windows in houses. All she could see was the brick wall next door. If she strained, she could see the road in front of the house and a corner of the back garden the other direction. She supposed the beautiful room more than made up for the poor view.

Nellie strolled around the room admiring the decorations. She'd be more comfortable here than in the closet of a bedroom she used at her aunt's house. As soon as she knew for sure she was staying, she'd send for the rest of her things. They'd probably look dowdy among all the other knick-knacks laying around. Satisfied she'd examined every part of her new bedroom, Nellie made her way to the drawing room where Mrs. McGowen sat in state, stroking her dog.

"Have you settled in your room?" she asked when Nellie had taken the seat Mrs. McGowen indicated. "Is everything to your satisfaction?"

"Yes, ma'am. The room is lovely, the prettiest I've ever seen."

"Then you haven't traveled much." Mrs. McGowen sniffed and stared down her nose at the letter open on the table next to her chair. "I hardly know how to occupy your time while you're here. I don't know what Warren was thinking inviting you to stay."

"He said you needed companionship."

"It isn't for him to say what I need or don't need. Still, as long as you're here you could read me this letter. The woman in charge of the luncheon at the country club uses the most flowery handwriting imaginable. I simply can't make it out. Let's see how you fare."

Nellie took the offered paper and glanced over it. The lettering *was* flowery, more so than normal. But it wasn't illegible. She read aloud the invitation to a luncheon to be held in a month and information about the charity they were assisting this year. When she finished, she handed the letter back to Mrs. McGowen.

"I don't know why they insist on inviting me every year. I can never attend."

Nellie frowned. "Why can't you attend? It's for a good cause."

"I'm too old. The food they fix is too rich for my taste. They're a bunch of gossiping old biddies who can't keep their opinions to themselves."

Nellie decided to put a cheerful face on it. She tinkled a laugh. "You should go and prove those old biddies wrong."

"Prove them wrong? How, exactly? Especially since I can't walk into the event without help and I won't be able to eat anything."

"You're proving them wrong simply by attending." Nellie's smile had faded to a strained imitation of what it had been.

"I'm not attending. I never attend."

"Why couldn't you go this once? For a change of scenery if nothing else. How long has it been since you left the house?"

Mrs. McGowen glared at her. "Why do you want to know? Are you afraid you've doomed yourself to spend months, no, years cooped up in a house with an old woman?"

Nellie glared back. "Why can't you leave the house? Why won't you? It would do you good. Your dog is getting fat with all food you feed it. You could walk it up the street and back for practice. In a month, you'll be able to sweep in there like you own the place. It would give those old gossips something to talk about for months to come."

"How dare you criticize me about how I care for my Sophia! She is the only person in the world who loves me for who I am. Unconditionally!" The old woman squeezed the dog. The dog yipped a complaint and tried to wriggle free. "Now see what you've done! She knows we're arguing."

"She doesn't love you for who you are. She loves you because you feed her all day, every day." Nellie wasn't even trying to be nice anymore. She didn't care.

The old woman jerked back like she'd been struck. Her chin quivered. She set the dog on the floor and struggled to her feet. "I'll be in my room if anyone needs me. I'll answer this letter tomorrow. They won't care if the reply comes the day after it was sent. They all call me eccentric to my face. Eccentric old women can get away with delaying their answer." Her voice finished with a sob and she staggered from the room. The dog waddled after her.

Nellie watched them leave. She was amazed Mrs. McGowen hadn't asked her to repack her things and leave right then. She crossed the room and picked up the letter. They didn't have to reply for a week. Why did she insist they needed to answer by return mail?

A roll-top desk stood in a corner of the drawing room. Nellie opened it. In the center cubby hole, she found Mrs. McGowen's stationery and a fountain pen. She'd been complimented on her handwriting her whole life. She could answer the letter, decline the invitation as Mrs. McGowen requested. Maybe she'd be pleased to hear Nellie had gotten it done today and sent in the afternoon post.

She began the letter but reached the part when she would decline. 'Regretfully, I find I must decline your invitation to the charity luncheon this year.' She stopped writing and stared at the words. Her pen hovered over the paper. A drop of ink fell onto the page, ruining it. She set the pen aside and considered.

What if? What if she was to accept the invitation and then inform Mrs. McGowen of her acceptance afterward? She stood and paced the room, considering the consequences. She knew the old woman would be angry. She'd be angry if someone did that to her.

But Nellie also knew she couldn't tolerate being stuck inside this stuffy house, this mausoleum of sorts, for the indefinite future. She whirled back to the desk and took out a fresh sheet of paper. She penned the letter in a matter of minutes, accepting the invitation. She addressed the envelope, went in search of the butler, and asked him to post it. A pleased satisfaction filled Nellie as she crumpled the ruined paper into a ball and threw it in the fire. Oh, she'd probably be in huge trouble when Mrs. McGowen found out. She might even be asked to leave. So be it. She'd deal with it when the time came.

A light tap sounded on the drawing room door. Nellie turned to see the butler, Reynolds, gazing into the room. "Luncheon is served, Miss Eleanor. Mrs. McGowen will not be joining you."

"Thank you, Reynolds. I'll be right there."

Nellie settled at the dining room table, thankful for the light chicken salad and toast the cook had made. Everything tasted so good.

There was a clatter of claws on the wood floor in the hall. Sophia appeared next to her chair and sat there, thumping her little tail against the floor. Nellie sighed.

"Are you hungry?"

The dog's tail thumped harder.

"Don't you have food in the kitchen? Come on. We'll check."

She stood and led the way through the door to the kitchen. The dog stopped outside it and wouldn't follow her.

Reynolds met them there. "Cook won't allow the dog in the kitchen. Says it isn't sanitary."

"I suppose it isn't. Where is she supposed to be fed?"

"The mistress feeds the dog off her plate."

Nellie frowned at this. "All the time? Without exception? The dog never eats out of her own dish?"

"She doesn't even have a dish for the dog. The veterinarian wanted us to use one but the mistress insisted otherwise."

Nellie stared at the dog staring back at her expectantly. "I supposed I'm expected to feed her since Mrs. McGowen isn't eating for lunch?"

"I don't know what's expected of you, Miss Eleanor. I can take the dog away if you want."

"No, leave her here with me. I'll figure it out."

She returned to her food in the dining room, followed by the dog who continued to watch her eat with hope-filled eyes. The little thing was so fat she could barely walk. Judging by how thin Mrs. McGowan was, the dog had probably been getting most of her food. Nellie sighed and slipped Sophia a taste of the chicken salad. Sophia ate it out of her hand, then looked up again, expectant. Nellie fed her a bite of toast. They continued this way until Nellie's plate was clean. When the dog saw she wasn't getting any more food, she licked her mouth clean and trotted back up the hall to Mrs. McGowen's room.

When Nellie reached the hall, she saw Mrs. McGowen's door was shut and the dog sat outside, whining to get in. The dog trotted over to Nellie and then back to the closed door.

Nellie didn't know if she should open the door and let the dog into the bedroom. Had Mrs. McGowan shut it out on purpose? She went in search of Reynolds once more.

"Does Mrs. McGowan have a lead for the dog somewhere?"

"It's hanging on a nail in the coat closet, though why she has it, I'll never know. She never goes outside."

"Thank you, Reynolds."

Nellie retrieved the lead and attached it to the dog's collar. Then she pulled on her coat and wrapped a scarf around her head. The day was sunny but cool and breezy. She hoped to find a small park like the one near her aunt's and uncle's house.

The dog followed her willingly for the first block, reluctantly for the second, then lagged behind for the third. Nellie kept having to stop and wait for the dog to catch up. Then it would sit and breathe hard for a minute before they could continue. At the end of the block, the dog sat down and refused to move.

"I am not carrying you the rest of the way," Nellie hissed at the animal. "You have legs. You can walk."

The dog stared up at her with pitiful eyes.

"I'll get your hair all over my coat!"

The dog moaned and rolled onto its side.

"We are almost home! Your house is right up there!" Nellie stepped away from the dog as far as the lead would allow and pointed.

With another moan, the dog struggled to its feet and trotted to the end of the block. When she saw her house, so close, she took off running. Nellie followed as fast as was proper for a woman to walk and clung to the lead with all her strength. The dog dashed up the front steps and into the door Reynolds held open for them.

"I see miss fatty there survived." Reynold's voice dripped with irony.

"She barely made it around the block." Nellie shrugged out of her coat and handed it to Reynolds. "I suppose she'll need a bath before we can let her back on any of the carpet."

"I suppose so." Reynolds hung the coat but made no move to do anything with the dog.

"I'll bathe her if you'll show me where to do it."

"Right this way, miss. And thank you. That dog needed to get out of this house."

Chapter Eight

While the three of them ate dinner, Sophia lay sprawled across the dining room floor, snoring.

"I have no idea what's gotten into her," said Mrs. McGowen, watching her dog with concern. "She never sleeps like this. She's up at all hours of the day and night."

Nellie tried to contain her grin. She focused on her plate instead of on the sleeping dog.

"How did you and Miss Greene get along today, Aunt?" asked Warren.

But the old woman couldn't concentrate on anything except the dog. "Do I need to phone the veterinarian?"

"She's fine," Nellie broke into the conversation. "I took her for a walk after lunch. It must have worn her out."

Mrs. McGowen looked horrified. "She hasn't eaten anything since! She's going to be hungry and keep me up all night. And what about all the dirt and germs she encountered out there! She'll get sick and die and then where will I be?" The old woman choked on a sob.

"There, there, Aunt. She's fine. Many dogs live long, healthy lives outdoors."

"But Sophia isn't accustomed to it," Mrs. McGowen whined.

"I gave her a bath when we came back," said Nellie. "We can make a small dish of food for her to eat before bed. She shouldn't disturb you tonight."

Mrs. McGowen's eyes narrowed. "I don't appreciate you going behind my back like this. I don't care what you think your job here is, you have no business harming my dog. Or interfering in anything else for that matter."

"Then I suppose I should probably not tell you I accepted the invitation to the charity luncheon next month. I told them you would be attending with a guest."

Mrs. McGowen threw her napkin on the table and stood. Her chair scraped loudly across the wood floor, waking the dog. "How dare you! When I specifically said we would not be going. You will write back to them immediately and tell them there was a mistake and I won't be attending, like I said when we talked."

Nellie stood as well, and faced the old woman. "I will not stay here, inside this house, without going anywhere, for the indefinite future. If that's how you expect it to be, I'm leaving tonight." She dropped her napkin next to her own plate and turned to leave.

Mr. Burke stood. "Ladies. Please. Sit. Let's discuss this before any of us do anything rash."

Mrs. McGowen sank into her chair, followed by Nellie. The dog settled back on the floor and, moments later, resumed snoring.

As far as Nellie could see, Mrs. McGowen hadn't eaten a bite of her food. She was starting to suspect the old woman didn't eat. Instead, she gave her food to the dog to give the illusion she'd eaten.

"Aunt, you know the veterinarian has been telling you to take the dog for a walk for months now. You are feeding your dog to death and not providing it with any exercise."

"And she's not eating anything herself," Nellie said, blurting the words before she'd fully thought about it.

Mr. Burkes' eyebrows flew upward. "Is this true, Aunt?" He scrutinized her plate. His eyes widened when he saw how much of her food was left. "Have you been feeding most of your food to the dog?"

"The food Cook fixes is too rich for me. If I eat anything I get fatter. Or at the very least, I get indigestion."

"You could have indigestion because you never eat."

"I eat! Just not as much as this cow over here." She waved at Nellie. "No wonder she couldn't find a husband."

Nellie sprang to her feet. Her face was hot but she couldn't tell if it was from anger or embarrassment. Maybe both. She threw her napkin onto the table again and ran from the room. She didn't care if she was ladylike or not. She took the stairs two at a time, dashed into her new bedroom, and slammed the door behind her.

She paced the room, shaking with anger. Oddly, she didn't feel like crying. She thought back to a conversation she'd had with Gran a couple years before. She'd behaved foolishly and Gran had told her. She'd called Nellie a silly, foolish girl. Nellie had said things back to Gran in anger, defended herself. Later, she'd seen Gran had been right all along. The last words Nellie had ever spoken to her Gran had been those spoken in anger.

Guilt washed over Nellie as it always did when she remembered her Gran. Most of the time she tried to quash the emotion. She couldn't ignore it tonight. She would have saved herself years of heartache if she'd listened to Gran's warning. She would have noticed Philip Coburg's lack of interest months earlier. Maybe things would have turned out differently with Edward. Both times she'd pushed for her own way. Both times she'd been horribly mistaken.

Nellie's pacing slowed. She thought over the conversation at the dinner table. An old woman was behaving foolishly and got angry when people called her on it. This old woman was so determined she was right, she was willing to starve herself to death to prove her point.

A horrible, sick sensation rolled over Nellie.

She would be like Mrs. McGowen when she got old, if she didn't start making changes right now, if she didn't start heeding her Gran's warning from years before. Silly, foolish girls who didn't change became silly, foolish old women. The evidence was sitting downstairs in the dining room.

She stared at her reflection in the dressing table mirror. She could see the same haughty eyes, the same stubborn line in her jaw she'd see in Mrs. McGowen's. The same lines between her eyebrows from frowning when she didn't get her way. She jerked back and passed her hands over her face. How had she never noticed this before?

And how, oh! how could she go about changing before it was too late?

Chapter Nine

Warren stood outside Nellie's bedroom door and hesitated. No sounds emitted from inside. Had she gone to bed? Should he disturb her? His aunt had agreed to be civil and he wanted to take advantage of this shift in mood. He raised his fist to knock.

The door swung open before he touched it. Nellie gave a startled cry, then clapped her hand over her mouth, eyes wide. She schooled her features on a soft laugh. "You startled me, Mr. Burke. I didn't expect you to be standing there."

"Yes. Well. My aunt has agreed to talk about what happened. She's promised to listen to your point of view. I feel we should take advantage of this since she never makes concessions to anyone."

"I was on my way down to talk to her, too."

Warren stepped out of the doorway and led the way down stairs. Aunt Louellen awaited them in the drawing room. Sophia slept curled at her feet. The little dog twitched now and then, but otherwise didn't move.

Nellie stood stiffly in the middle of the floor, her hands clenched in the folds of her dress. Warren expected her to lift her chin and rail on his aunt. His aunt probably deserved it.

Instead, she faced the old woman and remained calm. "I should not have responded to the invitation the way I did. I should have observed your request to decline it. I will write a retraction tonight and send it in the early post tomorrow morning.

"As for the dog, she was trying to return to your room after luncheon. I thought you might be sleeping and I didn't want to disturb you. The weather was lovely, so I took her for a walk because I wanted to get out of the house."

Aunt Louellen refrained from saying a word the whole time Nellie was speaking. She said nothing until Nellie had taken a seat across from her and Warren had joined them.

"I suppose it won't kill Sophia to get out now and then. Warren has been reminding me of the veterinarians warning the last time he was here. He said she'd be dead within the year if I didn't take her for exercise and change her diet. I don't know how I can change her diet, so we'll have to try the exercise." She leaned over to stroke the dog, who didn't move except to twitch an ear.

"But I must insist you rescind your acceptance of the invitation. My constitution will not allow me to leave the house any more. I'll finish my days in this house and probably never step a foot outside it."

"That's rather fatalistic, wouldn't you say, Aunt?" said Warren.

"It may be fatalistic, but it's true."

"It doesn't have to be true." Now Nellie's chin *was* lifted. Her eyes met his aunts with a stubbornness that matched her own. Warren was impressed.

"Don't be silly, child. Who expects any more of a woman my age?"

"I'm not a child," said Nellie. "My Gran stayed active until the last weeks of her life. She wanted to go out and do things. If you *decide* you want to do something, you'll be able to do it."

Warren watched his aunt for her reaction. He expected to her explode in anger, as she was prone to do. He expected her to lash out at Nellie. She stayed silent.

"Give this one event a try. If you hate it, or it doesn't go well, we'll never do anything like it again. What do you have to lose?" Nellie continued, refusing to back down.

"I have plenty to lose — my health for one. What if I catch pneumonia at the luncheon?"

"I know a good doctor who can treat you."

"What if I fall and break a bone?"

"You won't. I'll help you every step of the way. Everything you need is on this level in your house. I'll be here to nurse you until you can walk again. Besides, you could take the dog for walks. For practice. It might improve your appetite."

"My appetite is fine." Aunt Louellen glared at Warren, instead of Nellie.

Nellie shot him a puzzled frown. Warren gave a small jerk of his head. He'd have to let her know what was behind that glare after his aunt went to bed.

"I'll consider it." The old woman absently stroked the dog once more. "But I'm tired of talking about this. Go to the kitchen, Eleanor, and see if Cook and Reynolds obeyed my order. This dog needs food. I want you to supervise her feeding while I prepare for bed." She stood, clinging to the arms of the chair to keep her balance. Leaning on the cane, she shuffled to her room. Sophia woke, stretched with a huge yawn, and followed.

"What happened after I left?" Nellie asked once his aunt was gone.

"I sat there and made her eat some of her food. She wasn't happy with me. I'd noticed she was getting thinner and the dog fatter, but I didn't make the connection she was feeding her food to the dog so she wouldn't have to eat it."

"I can't understand her reasoning. The cook fixes such lovely food. I can't imagine not wanting to eat it."

"Ah, see that's where you'd be wrong. My aunt's old cook quit. She was quite old herself and couldn't stand the long hours in the kitchen. My aunt was angry about the change and went through three cooks in rapid succession because she insisted their food was terrible. I found this new cook. The wages she was asking were reasonable. Her food is delicious. I told my aunt if she fired the woman, I'd never come to stay with her again. It appears my aunt has been refusing to eat the food this cook prepares as some sort of protest against me. After you went upstairs, she told me since she couldn't fire her, she decided not to eat the food."

"Your aunt would starve herself to death out of spite?" Nellie felt the same shock and horror she'd felt earlier, followed by the same guilt. She wasn't much different than Mrs. McGowen.

"I don't think it would have come to that. We humans have an innate need to preserve ourselves. I think she wanted to make herself sick and blame the cook so I'd have to fire her. Ultimately, she'd get her own way."

Nellie shook her head. She stood and started for the door. "I'd better go check on the dog food like she asked."

Warren stood and followed. "I insisted we change the eating arrangements for the dog. She can't be eating off my aunt's plate anymore. Cook won't allow the dog in the kitchen for obvious reasons. I suggested we place a dish on a heavy cloth or towel in the dining room and allow her to eat there. She can even eat during meal times. But she must eat out of her own dish. She has a silver dish she never uses."

"I'm glad to hear it. Reynolds told me they didn't have a dish for the dog."

"Aunt Louellen kept it in her room and refused to let the dog use it. I found it earlier and gave it to Reynolds."

Sophia appeared in the dining room doorway. She trotted over to the dish Reynolds had placed on a cloth. She sniffed the contents once, then devoured them in a matter of minutes.

"Looks like the dog doesn't mind the new arrangements," said Nellie as the dog trotted back out of the room.

"She's happy as long as she gets fed," said Warren.

"Come, I have something I want to show you," said Warren once his aunt was in bed. He lead the way to the room he used as a study while in town.

"I don't know if you like to read. If not, you can come in here on days when the weather is too poor to go for a walk to get some space from my aunt. But you are welcome to read any of the books in this room. You can take them to your bedroom, as long as you return them when you're done."

Nellie spun in place taking in the floor to vaulted ceiling shelves filled with books. "This is amazing."

"I didn't accumulate all these books on my own. Some of them belonged to my father and grandfather and are quite old. I also enjoy the occasional pulp fiction while I'm traveling. Those volumes are here."

Nellie saw rows of books by Edgar Allen Poe, Arthur Conan Doyle, and Charles Dickens. "My school library had Sherlock Holmes mysteries. He's so clever. I think I'll start there." She pulled a volume from the shelf.

"Do you enjoy reading?" Warren asked, wanting to see her response as much as hear it.

"Not as much as I should," she said. "Not as much as you." She waved her hand at the rows of volumes, then threw him a smile over her shoulder.

Her smile sent the oddest sensation fluttering through Warren's stomach. He wondered if he could get her to smile at him like that again. Something had happened between when she'd stormed out of the dining room and when she'd come back downstairs. She'd been closed off, careful, only allowing him and his aunt to see what she wanted them to see. Now, there was an openness that hadn't been there before. A…genuineness and humility, for lack of better words to describe it. Warren liked what he saw now. He hoped she could last as his aunt's companion. He hoped he'd get to see her, spend time with her, between business trips.

"Does your aunt enjoy reading?"

"I honestly don't know. I doubt her eyesight is good enough for her to read much these days. She has spectacles but rarely uses them."

"Would she be interested if I offered to read to her? The days are too long for her to pass all of them lying in bed."

"You'll have to discuss it with her. She claims she's read all the books in this library she's interested in reading. Maybe you know of something she would find tempting. It can't hurt to ask.

"Now, there are some matters of business we need to discuss. More accurately, of which you need to be aware, since I'll be gone for the next several weeks."

Warren walked behind the desk and took a seat, indicating Nellie sit in one of the chairs facing the desk. Warren pulled a ledger from the center drawer and opened it where they could both see it.

"My aunt's solicitor disperses the salaries of all the employees, including you. I don't know what kind of remuneration you were expecting..."

Shocked, Nellie held up a hand and interrupted him. "I wasn't expecting remuneration, pay, compensation, whatever."

"Yes. Well. You can't be expected to live here and perform your duties for free. I've allotted a certain amount in the budget for you. You'll receive it at the beginning of the month along with the other employees.

"My aunt receives a monthly stipend as well. The solicitor will bring it and leave it here in the safe." Warren stood and showed Nellie how to open the safe, revealing several months worth of funds. "As you can see, my aunt uses very little of the money allotted. She buys food, pays some bills - though I think the solicitor takes care of those when he comes as well."

Warren closed the safe and returned to the desk. "You are allowed to use this money for my aunt's needs or wants. If she wants to eat out, or buy a new hat or gloves. If you want different books than the ones contained in this library."

"I can't imagine needing different books..." Nellie began.

Warren raised his hand and stopped her. "My aunt's taste may not run the same as yours. You might also find something, a book, she would find more entertaining than what is provided here." He couldn't keep the eager twinkle from his eye. "Books are a necessity and there's never a good excuse not to buy them."

Nellie chuckled at his enthusiasm.

Warren grew serious again. "I would love it if you could get her out of the house and mixing with people again. But even if you can't, if you can help her enjoy what time she has left on this earth, I would be grateful."

"I'll do the best I can, but that's a tall order."

"I know. I gave up on it years ago. It's hypocritical for me to expect something of you I'm unable to fulfill myself. However, observing the things I have tonight, I feel you are up to the task. You may be better suited to it than anyone we've attempted so far."

Nellie frowned, flushed with embarrassment and stared at the floor. Warren feared he'd offended her. "I'm not sure if that's a compliment or not," she finally said.

"I intended it as such."

Nellie's gaze met his and she gave him that smile again. His stomach fluttered oddly again. He couldn't tear his eyes away from hers. Nellie's blush deepened.

A knock sounded at the open door and they both turned to see who it was.

Reynolds poked his head in the door. "I'm leaving for the night."

"Thank you, Reynolds. We'll see you tomorrow."

Once the butler had left, Warren struggled to remember what else he needed to tell Nellie before he left. She broke the silence first.

"How do I reach you if there's an emergency?"

"I'll leave contact information, where I'm lodging, where to telephone or send telegrams. A telegram will often be the fastest way to reach me. Reynolds or the solicitor can help you if you are unable to do it yourself. In the worst circumstances, you can make an overseas telephone call. But those are unreliable and you'll have to keep in mind the time difference if you make them.

"I won't keep you any longer tonight. Thank you, again, for taking care of my aunt. She may not appreciate it yet, but I certainly do."

Nellie grabbed her book and disappeared upstairs. He could hear her walking around her bedroom, right above the study. He'd made enquiries about her over the last couple days. He knew little of her history before she'd arrived in Boston a couple years before. Since then, she'd been in the middle of two different scandals involving men. He'd determined she was an injured party in both situations.

He sat back and considered Aunt Louellen and all the scandals following her in her youth. He'd heard tales but didn't know if any of them were true. These two women were peas in a pod. He hoped it would work to their benefit and not their detriment. One thing was certain, Nellie was stubborn enough to withstand anything his aunt threw at her.

Chapter Ten

Warren sailed for Europe the following week, and the days stretched before them in endless monotony. Nellie hadn't seen him much when he was in town. He'd only been around in the evenings. But that tiny respite meant the full burden of entertaining Mrs. McGowen wasn't on her shoulders alone.

It didn't help wet weather had moved in and it had been rainy and cold for days. Nellie stared out the parlor window at the soggy street.

"Eleanor!"

Mrs. McGowen was trying to decipher the crossword puzzle in a women's magazine she received in the post the previous day. She'd been plugging away at it ever since. The trouble was, she relied on Nellie to provide most of the answers.

"Yes, Mrs. McGowen?"

"Number four down. Clue is 'manner of movement'. Four spaces. I think I put the wrong word in the other day."

"Try 'gait'," Nellie suggested.

Reynolds stepped into the parlor doorway.

"Were you desiring the car for an outing today, miss?"

Nellie frowned. An outing was the last thing on her mind. She almost said as much, when something occurred to her. “You said Cook is out sick today, Reynolds?”

“Yes, miss. She came for breakfast but had to leave. She said she couldn’t even smell what she was cooking so what was the point.”

Nellie hid a smile. She couldn’t disagree with the logic. She hurried out of the parlor. Grabbing Reynolds by the sleeve, she pulled him into the dining room. “Do you think Mrs. McGowen would be willing to go out for lunch or dinner?”

“She hasn’t left the house in…” Reynolds hesitated. “It might be years now, miss. Except those walks you have her taking with the dog the last few days.”

“I’ll let you know about the car. I’m going to try to talk her into going out for a change. Is there food for the dog in the kitchen?”

“I’ll see what I can find.” Reynolds disappeared through the dining room, while Nellie returned to the parlor.

“There you are.” Mrs. McGowen scowled at her. “I’ve been calling you. What took you so long? Where did you go? I can’t figure out a six letter word meaning ‘the heart of the home’.

“Hearth,” said Nellie absently. “Did Reynolds tell you the cook was out sick today?”

“Of course he did. I’d be out sick from this infernal rain, if I wasn’t already stuck at home with it.” Mrs. McGowen’s scowl deepened.

“You never leave home anyway,” Nellie reminded her. “But we could remedy that today. I asked Reynolds to have the car sent around. We’re going out for lunch.”

The old woman drew herself up. Shock flickered across her face, followed by a look of horror. "How could you make such an arrangement without consulting me first?"

Nellie glanced at the door in time to see Reynolds scurrying for the telephone in the study. He was calling the car.

"I'm sure there's plenty of food in the house and we'd be fine on our own. But, before he left, Mr. Burke told me he thought it would be nice if you got out more. He suggested going out for lunch now and then. The cook makes better food than anything we'd get in a restaurant. So, since she's not here, today seems like the perfect day to give it a try."

"I don't have anything to wear."

"That's not true. I've seen your wardrobe. It's packed full of clothes you never wear because you never leave the house."

"It's too cold. I'll catch my death of pneumonia out there."

"We'll bundle you up nice and warm. You can walk straight to the car under an umbrella and straight into the restaurant the same way. You won't even notice the cold or the rain. I can have my father come check you when we get home if you're still worried."

"What will Sophia eat?"

"Reynolds already checked. There's food in the kitchen for her. We can watch to make sure she eats before we leave. Reynolds will be here the whole time we're gone. She'll probably sleep anyway."

"You've thought of everything, haven't you?" Mrs. McGowen didn't even attempt to keep the bitter edge out of her voice.

"I won't take 'no' for an answer, if that's what you mean," said Nellie.

Mrs. McGowen sniffed loudly. "Let's change clothes. We can't go anywhere decent dressed like this."

An hour later, the dog had been fed and both women had changed clothes. Nellie helped Mrs. McGowen into her coat and wrapped a scarf around her neck. She shrugged into her own coat and hat. Reynolds waited for them by the door with an umbrella.

Mrs. McGowen stepped outside the front door. She hesitated. "I don't know if I can do this." Her voice shook.

"Come, madam," said Reynolds. "We can't stand here. I'll get you settled in the car and come back for Miss Greene."

"You're in on this, aren't you?"

"I think it's high time you let someone talk you into leaving the house." Reynolds placed a hand at Mrs. McGowen's elbow and half escorted, half pulled her down the short walk to the car.

Nellie followed without waiting for the umbrella. Reynolds held it higher so she could slip inside the car door. He closed it behind them and scurried back up the walk.

"Where do you want to go, Mrs. McGowen?" asked the driver.

Mrs. McGowen settled regally into the seat and drew a heavy robe left there from the winter over her lap. "Take us to the Parker House Hotel."

Nellie's eyebrows shot up. She hadn't planned on anything so fancy. "My original idea was to go to a small restaurant I know of not far from here. The food and service are good."

"If I'm going to leave the house for the first time in years, I want to eat at Parker House. My husband had a table there for many years. I'm sure they no longer hold it for me. But once they know who I am, they'll seat us first."

Nellie hoped that was the case.

Mrs. McGowen continued. "Have you ever eaten at Parker House, Eleanor?"

"Yes, ma'am," Nellie said. "Once."

"Only once?"

"I prefer eating in…" She hesitated, searching for the word to describe how she felt, "…less fussy restaurants."

"Parker House isn't fussy," sniffed Mrs. McGowen.

The two women fell silent. Nellie watched the buildings roll by her window. Everything was soggy. A few men and women picked their way over muddy sidewalks and streets. Otherwise, the usually bustling roads were quiet. Everyone had decided to stay inside on this cloudy, rainy day.

The car stopped in front of the huge building. The doorman hurried to the car with an umbrella and helped them out. He escorted them inside the foyer. Nellie tried not to stare at the marble interior, shiny after the dim, rainy outdoors.

"Can I take your coat, Mrs. McGowen?" asked a liveried bellboy, who wasn't a boy at all but a gray-haired old man. "It's a pleasure to see you again, after so long. You're looking well."

"Thank you. I'll keep my coat. It doesn't feel much warmer in here than it did outside." Mrs. McGowen stared down her nose at the man, despite his kind words.

Nellie shrugged out of her coat and handed it to the bellboy with an apologetic smile. She immediately regretted her decision to remove her coat. Mrs. McGowen was correct, the foyer was chilly.

Mrs. McGowen swept into the dining room and stopped next to the maitre 'd. "I'd like a table for two."

The man looked up from the paper he was reading, eyes wide. "Mrs. McGowen. It's a…It's a pleasure," he stammered. He stuffed the paper away somewhere. "Of course I can get you to a table right away. Please, follow me."

Nellie had never seen anything like Mrs. McGowen's haughty indifference to the service staff around her. Waiters seated them, filled water glasses, spread napkins on their laps, and listed the specials of the day. Mrs. McGowen ordered in French for both of them. The wait staff disappeared as quickly as they'd appeared.

"This is a lovely idea, Eleanor. I'm so glad you insisted. You're right. The thought of eating their food is waking my appetite in a spectacular way. We must try their cream pie for dessert. I hear it's legendary."

Nellie took in the near-empty dining room. "Is business always this slow?" she asked.

"Don't be crass. Of course not. It must be the weather."

Silence stretched between them. Nellie fought against the urge to fiddle with the napkin or cutlery. She finally had an idea.

"You said you had a table reserved here with your husband. Where was it?"

"It wasn't a particular table. My husband ate here so often if he came in, they'd give him preference over those who'd arrived earlier, even if they had reservations. We ate here several times a week. I continued the tradition for many years after his death."

Mrs. McGowen had never spoken of her husband. Nellie was curious. "What was your husband's business?"

"Imports and exports. It's the same business Warren manages today. His father took over after my husband's death. My brother and my husband were business partners. It's how we met. Warren took over the business after his father's death. We are all the family left to each other."

"That's so sad," Nellie said. "You never had children?"

"No! Of course not! Not that it's any of your business if I did. I never wanted children and Theodore never insisted. We weren't married long. He only lived ten years after we married. There have been times I wished I had children to pass along the family name, but one can't live in regret. Besides, I have Warren."

They watched the waiters make their way across the dining room with the first course. Mrs. McGowen ate in silence. Nellie followed her example. She watched in fascination as the food disappeared from Mrs. McGowen's plate without the aid of the dog. The final course - the cream pie, was the most delicious dessert Nellie had ever tasted. She was already full before they brought it out and only had room for a small taste. But the taste was enough to convince her to eat as much of the rest as her stomach would hold. She sat back and sighed with contentment when she finished.

Mrs. McGowen had a whispered conversation with the maitre'd, then stood to leave. Nellie thanked the waiters and complimented the cook in hushed tones then hurried after her elderly companion.

The bellboy was waiting in the foyer with her coat, as if he'd been standing there holding it the whole time. Nellie wondered for a second if he had. He held it while she slid her arms into the sleeves. Then the doorman escorted them to the waiting car. Had it been idling by the curb the entire time?

"We didn't pay," Nellie said in a near whisper.

"One should never speak of money in polite society." Mrs. McGowen lifted her chin and stared down her nose out the window.

"One should always pay their debts," Nellie returned.

"I have a standing tab at the hotel. The bill will be sent to my solicitor who will pay it for me."

"Ah." Nellie thought back to her conversation with Mr. Burke and understood. She wished she'd asked for more details about which bills the solicitor paid. It would have saved some worry and embarrassment.

The rain had slowed to a drizzle as they cruised along the city streets. Nellie saw a bookstore not far ahead. She leaned forward and tapped on the driver's seat. "Pull over there! I want to see what they have."

"Eleanor! We've been gone for hours. Sophia will be worried. What can you be thinking?"

"I want a book to read."

"We have books at home."

"We have a whole room full of books, yes, but I want a book to read to *you*. One I think you'll enjoy. When was the last time you read a book?"

The old lady scowled at her. Then her features softened. "It's been far too long. My eyes aren't as good as they once were. Fine. Pull over here. Apparently, we're book shopping."

The driver helped them out and escorted them to the book shop door. A bell tinkled when they entered the dim room. Nellie closed the door behind them and stopped. She took in a lung full of the smell of paper.

"Isn't that the best smell in the whole world?" she whispered. She slipped her arm through Mrs. McGowen's and led the way along the shelves.

"Can I help you?" asked a voice from behind them.

Nellie glanced over her shoulder. A bespectacled man stood at a counter on the opposite side of the shop from the door.

"We're looking for a book," she said. She flushed as soon as the words left her mouth.

Mrs. McGowen coughed into her handkerchief. Nellie could see something in the old woman's eyes she had never seen there before. Was that a twinkle of humor? Was she laughing at Nellie's gaffe?

"Obviously," said the clerk, barely containing his eye roll. "This *is* a book shop. Let me know if you find what you're searching for."

Mrs. McGowen coughed into her handkerchief again. This time Nellie could see the smile she was trying to hide.

"'*We're looking for a book*'?" the old woman hissed.

Nellie shrugged, but struggled to hide her own embarrassed laughter. "I was trying to narrow it down."

Mrs. McGowen barked a laugh, but it sounded strangled and unused. She attempted to disguise it by coughing once more but she hadn't fooled Nellie. A satisfied feeling spread through Nellie's chest. She'd gotten this cranky old lady to laugh for the first time in…well, who knew how long. Her smile turned smug.

"Excuse me," called a woman's voice from behind them.

Nellie had been scanning the shelves, not paying attention to what she was seeing. She turned and, this time, saw an older woman approaching.

"I'm sorry for my son's rude behavior. He manages my accounts but isn't good with people. Can I help you? Are you trying to find anything in particular?" The woman waited expectantly.

"We have a large library at home with every classic of literature you can imagine. It even has some more modern, Victorian era works. I was wondering if you have anything new, anything unusual you can recommend to help two women pass the evenings?"

Mrs. McGowen nodded her approval of Nellie's request. The two of them stood, waiting, still arm in arm.

"We just got several new books. Here's one that came in a few days ago by a brand new author. I have to confess I already read it. Simply couldn't put it down."

Nellie took the blue, hardcover book from the lady. It said: *The Mysterious Affair at Styles* by Agatha Christie.

The book shop matron wasn't finished. She leaned in conspiratorially and stage whispered, "It's quite thrilling and the detective sounds so handsome and distinguished."

Nellie shrugged and placed the volume on the counter. "Then we'll take it. Thank you for the recommendation."

She paid for the book and they left the shop. Mrs. McGowen was leaning on her arm, though less heavily than before. The driver helped them into the car and took them home.

Sophie greeted them at the door, a furry, wiggling, mess of yips, and sloppy dog kisses. Nellie wouldn't let the dog anywhere near her face, but Mrs. McGowen was happy for the love and attention. She baby talked to the dog all the way back to her bedroom where she closed herself inside for the rest of the afternoon.

Nellie placed the book on a table in the drawing room. She retrieved the Sherlock Holmes collection from the study and curled up on the couch to read. Her eyes were repeatedly drawn back to the paper-wrapped bundle on the end table.

Gathering up the last shred of self control she possessed, she extricated herself from the couch and went to her room. It was the only way she'd be able to leave the book alone until she could read it to Mrs. McGowen.

Chapter Eleven

The day of the ladies' aid luncheon was warm and humid.

"I don't know if I'll be able to attend," complained Mrs. McGowen. She fluttered a handkerchief at her flushed face, then dabbed her forehead with it. "It's not ladylike to perspire in public."

"I don't see what being ladylike has to do with perspiration," Nellie muttered under her breath as she carried the dog back to the cloth to eat for the second time that morning. Mrs. McGowen refused to eat anything, claiming the heat made her feel ill. Nellie had eaten, but she wished she hadn't. She felt out of sorts, not exactly sick, but not well. She suspected nerves more than anything. For both of them.

"We have to go. We can't give them something else to say about us." Nellie flopped onto the couch in a decidedly unladylike way. She didn't even care anymore. They had three hours to fill until it was time to leave. They both had to dress, but that wouldn't take the whole time.

"Read to me," demanded Mrs. McGowen.

Normally her tone would have annoyed Nellie, but Nellie knew how she felt. She picked up their book from the side table, opened to her marker, and began.

They'd finished the Agatha Christie mystery in a few days. Once they started, they'd devoured it as if their life depended on it. Nellie hadn't wanted to buy a new book every few days, especially when they had a room filled floor to ceiling with them. So she'd searched the library for books they already owned that Mrs. McGowen hadn't read. Mrs. McGowen had never been much of a reader and she was happy to hear anything Nellie thought worthwhile so it had been simple to find options.

Nellie had read the Sherlock Holmes mysteries, and, though Mrs. McGowen deemed them common and vulgar, she'd tried to figure out the clues as fast as Nellie read them. She would perch on the edge of her seat and stroke the dog until Sophia wriggled away from her. Then they'd read Edgar Allen Poe and Nathaniel Hawthorn. Mrs. McGowen claimed *House of Seven Gables* gave her nightmares and every crow in the neighborhood was waiting for its chance to peck her eyes out. She refused to leave the house for days and Nellie had been forced to walk the dog alone.

Nellie didn't mind walking the dog. They usually began their walk, all of them together. Nellie would complete a circuit of the block while Mrs. McGowen walked once up and down their street and waited outside the house for them to return.

A loud snore jerked Nellie's attention from the book she was reading. Mrs. McGowen's head was propped in the corner of her chair and she was fast asleep.

Nellie laid aside the book, a Louisa May Alcott book she'd never read before, and went in search of the dog. She could give Sophia a walk and be back in time to dress for the luncheon.

Nellie returned a few minutes later, now dripping with sweat herself, to hear Mrs. McGowen's screams from her bedroom.

Reynolds met her at the front door and took the dog's lead. "You'd better get in there, Miss. Fast. Chloe's threatened to walk out once already."

Nellie rushed back to the bedroom and pushed the door open. Mrs. McGowen, in her dressing gown, was shaking a wadded up gown in Chloe's face. "I told you I wanted the gray lawn!" she screamed again.

Chloe's eyes met Nellie's and for the first time Mrs. McGowen turned her attention away from the maid.

"She will not follow orders. She's insufferable! How can I expect to look decent in front of all those gossips if she doesn't know how to dress me?"

Nellie crossed the room and took the wadded dress from Mrs. McGowen. She shook it out and examined it. "I don't understand what is happening. Is this what she prepared for you to wear this afternoon?"

"Yes! And it's all wrong!"

"The invitation said we were to wear white. They wear white to the event every year. It's their uniform, I think. If you wear the gray, you'll be dressed differently than everyone there, including me."

"I don't care what they think! I don't care about formality or tradition. Their traditions are ridiculous and should be ended." The old woman broke into sobs, her entire body shaking, and sank into her dressing table chair.

Nellie wrapped her arms around the old woman and let her cry onto her shoulder.

"What is really bothering you, Mrs. McGowen?"

The woman straightened. "I used to be someone in these groups." She struck the dressing table with her fist. "They looked to me for help organizing the event and for financial backing. Now I'm an afterthought. They invite me out of a sense of duty and are secretly hoping I don't come. Which is the reason why I haven't attended for years now."

Nellie waved Chloe forward. The girl began brushing Mrs. McGowen's silky, white hair. Nellie watched her relax under the brush strokes. Nellie brought a wet cloth and wiped Mrs. McGowen's face and neck with it. She washed away all evidence of the tears. Mrs. McGowen grabbed her wrist and stopped the soothing actions.

"What if we get there and no one will talk to me?"

"They wouldn't dare."

Mrs. McGowen searched Nellie's face. Nellie tried to reassure her with a smile, though her own stomach was tied in knots at the prospect of facing the very ladies whom she'd overheard talking about her at the ball.

"Besides, they'll be talking about me, not you."

Mrs. McGowen dropped her hand into her lap and faced the mirror. "You mean because you've been jilted?"

It hadn't come up since the first day Nellie was here. She didn't feel like talking about it now.

"We are quite the pair, aren't we?" Mrs. McGowen actually smiled. "We both have things in our past they want to gossip about. Let's go and show them what we're made of today, shall we Eleanor? Because if I've learned anything about you, it's that you're made of much stiffer stuff than you let on."

"Was that a compliment?" Nellie asked with a giggle.

Mrs. McGowen glared back. "Giggling isn't ladylike."

"You don't think anything is ladylike anymore. Get dressed in the white dress Chloe laid out for you. I'll be down in a few minutes wearing my own white dress. We'll take that luncheon by storm."

∞

Nellie's feeling of dread increased the closer they came to the dining room. Mrs. McGowen had taken her arm and the two women approached the dining room door together.

"Are you ready for this?" Mrs. McGowen asked.

"As ready as I'll ever be," Nellie said.

The lady that greeted them barely concealed her surprise when she saw Mrs. McGowen. Nellie didn't know if it was surprise or shock. The lady had plastered a smile on her face.

"Mrs. McGowen. Miss Greene. We weren't sure if you were actually coming."

Mrs. McGowen looked down her nose at the lady and sniffed. "If I say I'll be in attendance, you can count on that fact, Hilda. I'm assuming you have assigned us a seat? I find standing quite tiring and would like to be shown there as soon as possible."

"Yes, of course," said Hilda. Nellie watched surprise, annoyance, and amusement flicker across the lady's face in turn and was thankful she didn't know what was behind those expressions.

The lady named Hilda called a waiter who escorted Nellie and Mrs. McGowen to their table. Nellie gazed across the dining area, which was, in reality, a huge, covered porch. As they crossed the room to their table, Mrs. McGowen grumbled that in her day, they would never have allowed the luncheon to be served al fresco. People didn't want flies in their food. Nellie didn't know how they'd accomplished it, but she had yet to see a single fly.

The group of women already seated fell silent when the two women arrived. The waiter seated them. Another filled their water glasses and settled their napkins across their laps.

Nellie watched Mrs. McGowen for clues how to act. The old lady gave each woman at the table a smile and folded her hands in her lap to wait.

"It's been a while, Louellen," said the woman across from Mrs. McGowen. "We weren't sure if you were still alive or if your obituary hadn't made it into the papers yet."

Mrs. McGowen's stiff smile focused on the woman. "I choose not to leave the house most of the time. I have everything I need there. My staff, my dog, my companion."

"Yes. Your companion," said another woman. She fiddled with the lace on her sleeve and wouldn't meet their eyes. "Interesting company you're keeping, I must say."

"You must say what, Elise? Have you been unable to find a companion to suit you now that your husband is deceased. But of course you couldn't. You wouldn't be able to find anyone to stand up to your sharp tongue."

"I'm surprised you were able to find someone to tolerate yours," said the first woman.

"Eleanor and I get on fine these days." Mrs. McGowen patted Nellie on the hand and smiled at her in what appeared to be her attempt at a motherly smile. Nellie wanted to wince and laugh at the same time. She wasn't wrong. They had been getting on quite well. Once they got past those first, rough, days.

"I assume she has told you nothing of her sketchy past." A third woman with a waspish appearance joined the conversation. "Like how she's a bit of the man chaser."

"Man chaser? She didn't say anything about it. I've not seen any questionable gentlemen hanging around, either. My nephew hired her and did a thorough background check. He found nothing obscene and questionable there. She did have relationships with two men that ended in misfortune. For both men, as I understand. Their misfortune had nothing to do with Eleanor here."

"That's not what I heard," the waspish woman retorted.

"Is that so? Then what exactly did you hear, Francine? Would you be so kind as to enlighten all of us so Eleanor here can answer the accusations made against her?"

Francine gave a furtive glance around the table at the other ladies. "I can't say. Not in polite company. It wouldn't be proper."

"But you can allude to it with impunity and without offending the same company, I see." Mrs. McGowen turned to Nellie. "Eleanor, would you be so kind as to inform these ladies of the exact nature of your relationship with Dr. Coburg?"

Nellie blinked in horror at the request. She'd been nothing but a flirt back then. She'd gone out of her way to throw herself at Dr. Coburg, with no regard for how he felt in the situation. She met Mrs. McGowen's frank gaze and knew she must tell the truth, no matter how it came across to these women.

"He came to my small town to help the elderly doctor left alone there when my father was here in Boston helping with the Spanish flu epidemic. He wanted a taste of the quiet country life. We became better acquainted when I fell ill with the Spanish flu and he treated me. I felt I'd fallen in love with him and thought he reciprocated the sentiment. But he left our town for a nearby city and became involved with a nurse there. He's since returned to Boston and married."

"You've not had any contact with him in the intervening time?"

Nellie felt like she was under a cross-examination. "No. None at all. He wanted nothing to do with me once he left our town."

"What about young Edward Reid? Did you have a relationship with him?"

"Yes. We were engaged for a time. His father wanted him to wait to get married until he'd established himself in the banking business. He even gave Edward a branch of his own in another town."

"Do you still have contact with this man?"

Nellie flushed deep red. She remembered the circumstances surrounding her falling out with Edward. Surely that had not been her fault? "No, of course not. We haven't been engaged in a long time. He's married to someone else now and I hear they have a baby. I haven't seen him since our engagement was broken off."

"He broke it off?"

Nellie wanted to crawl under the table. "No. His father did."

Mrs. McGowen faced the other women once more. "You see there. She has no terrible background with questionable young men to be ashamed of."

"She's been jilted twice," said the lady with the lace sleeves.

"Yes, Judy. Imagine how painful that must have been for her. Now, what are they serving at this luncheon? I hope they haven't let the standards slide since I was in charge of things here."

The women exchanged glances and fell silent. The waiter brought their first course, interrupting the awkwardness at the table.

Once the food had been served, the tasteful clatter of cutlery against china and the murmur of conversation was punctuated only by occasional laughter. The conversation at their table was stilted. Nellie didn't mind. She could see the other women were intimidated by Mrs. McGowen. They made a few polite attempts at conversation before it petered out and they ate in silence.

Mrs. McGowen didn't say much until they were in the car on the way home. They'd left as soon as they had fulfilled their social requirements. When they left, Mrs. McGowen swept from the room exactly as she had swept into it. She clung to Nellie's arm the whole way.

Nellie kept her back straight and head high, knowing the gossips at their table would fall into shameless conversation about them as soon as they were gone.

"Don't worry about those old biddies," said Mrs. McGowen into the hot silence of the car. "They have nothing better to do with their time than make up nasty stories about people intended to help them feel better about themselves. Who started all these rumors about you, anyway?"

"Edward's mother never liked me. She'd intended him for another girl. She and the girl's mother had everything worked out. She blamed me for what Edward did as soon as he moved away."

"What exactly did he do as soon as he moved away? No one has ever told me."

Nellie groaned. "Mrs. McGowen, please don't make me say it out loud. It isn't polite to talk about it. You're the one always insisting I be ladylike after all."

"Did he cause a woman to become with child outside of wedlock?" The old woman said the words without flinching or a hint of embarrassment. "It wouldn't be the first time a bachelor moved away and got lonely. I used to worry about Warren, but he barely seems to notice girls."

Mrs. McGowen reached across the upholstered seat and patted Nellie's hand. "You'd better start calling me Aunt Louellen like everyone else."

"Everyone else? Do you mean Mr. Burke?"

Mrs. McGowen laughed. It sounded like she was out of practice. "I suppose so. I suppose I shouldn't think it funny, either, but it is. Yes. I'd like it if both you and Warren would call me Aunt Louellen."

"I'd be happy to call you that, Aunt Louellen, especially after the luncheon today. You were amazing in there. I was proud to be in attendance with you."

The old woman's eyes filled with tears. She turned her gaze outside the window once more. Her fingers squeezed Nellie's before she returned them to her lap.

"My friends and family call me Nellie, not Eleanor," said Nellie hesitantly.

Aunt Louellen frowned at Nellie. "What a horrible moniker," she said. "Eleanor is so much better. My dearest friend in this life was named Eleanor. No, I won't call you by that awful nickname."

Mr. Burke had warned her, Nellie thought as she looked out her own window. She hid a grin. She didn't mind Mrs. McGowen...Aunt Louellen calling her Eleanor. A new name for a new beginning. It seemed appropriate.

She noticed storm clouds billowing in the distance. A breeze picked up and blew dust and a few straggling leaves across the road. Nellie closed her eyes and enjoyed the relief the cooler wind brought. It appeared they had, indeed, taken the luncheon by storm.

Chapter Twelve

Warren disembarked from the ocean liner at Boston Harbor in a rainstorm. He'd never been so happy to be on land in his life. He rarely got seasick. But the weather had been abysmal on this crossing and he'd spent most of the journey in his cabin. He'd sent his luggage with a porter earlier. Once he was off the boat, he made his way to Peters who waited next to his loaded car.

"Thank you, Peters. I assume everything is inside?"

"Yes, sir. I'm ready if you are."

Warren climbed into the vehicle and heaved a sigh of relief. He'd be right as rain in a day or two. Right now, he was so very tired.

The car slid through the wet Boston streets toward Aunt Louellen's house. If Warren was completely honest with himself, this trip had been harder because he'd been worried about her. He'd cut his travels short and come home early.

How was Aunt Louellen getting on with Nellie? Had they ever come to an understanding or were they still merely tolerating each other? He couldn't imagine Aunt Louellen tolerating Nellie for so many weeks. No, if she hadn't liked Nellie, she would have sent her away without a care about what Warren thought. She'd done that time and again with members of her staff he'd hired.

They parked in front of the house. Warren stepped out of the car into the steady drizzle. A moment later the front door was flung open. Reynolds hurried down the front walk with an umbrella. Nellie stood behind him, calling back into the house.

"He's arrived, Aunt Lou!"

Aunt Louellen entered the hall from the drawing room and bustled toward the front door. "Don't yell, Eleanor. It isn't ladylike."

"I wasn't yelling. I was informing you of his arrival."

"Hello, Aunt Louellen. I'm happy to see you looking so well." If Warren was completely honest, the entire tabloid he'd just witnessed was a relief. Nellie was still here. Aunt Louellen hadn't sent her away. They appeared to be getting along fine.

Aunt Louellen lifted her cheek for his kiss, then turned back to the drawing room. "Reynolds, please see the tea is brought to the drawing room for Mr. Burke. He's sure to be chilled through."

Nellie took Warren's overcoat from Reynolds as the butler hurried to the kitchen. She hung it in the coat closet. "It's good to see you, Mr. Burke. I hope your trip went well."

"It did. I had some trouble concentrating on my business. I was worried about how you were getting on here."

"You needn't have worried." Nellie threw him a smile over her shoulder and led the way to the drawing room.

Her smile caught Warren by surprise. He'd forgotten how lovely she was. He'd forgotten what a thrill he'd gotten out of earning those smiles once or twice before.

In that moment, he realized worry wasn't the only thing drawing him home early.

The thought made him scowl. Nellie's smile turned to a frown.

"Is everything alright, Mr. Burke?"

"Yes. I'm fine." Warren schooled his features and followed Nellie into the room.

"We were expecting you an hour ago," said Aunt Louellen.

"The fog delayed us. It took us longer to dock."

"I suspected that might be the case. I told Cook to hold tea until you arrived. Eleanor, please serve the cake. That's a dear."

Nellie had already begun cutting and serving the cake before Aunt Louellen said anything. She passed a plate to Warren and another to his aunt. Then she settled with her own next to his aunt on the couch.

"How have you ladies been?" he asked, hesitant. He felt like he needed to take everything slow, to feel out the relationship between these two.

"We've been well, thank you. Eleanor has been taking Sophia on walks and I've been joining them. Dr. Greene feels it's improved my constitution. I must take every care, given my advancing years."

She was fond of reminding him of her advancing years. Yet, this last had been a statement of fact, more out of a sense of habit or duty, than a means of making him feel guilty. Warren frowned again.

"Where is Sophia? I still haven't seen her. Is she well?" Warren had been half expecting his aunt to feed the dog some of her cake but the dog was no where to be seen.

The women exchanged a look.

"She's sleeping in the dining room by her food dish," Nellie explained. "We've found she eats and sleeps better if she takes her meals out of her own dish. She didn't eat well at lunch so I think she's hoping dinner comes early."

Was his aunt hiding an amused smile behind her napkin? Nellie wasn't even trying to hide her grin. Warren glanced from one woman to the other. What had happened while he was gone?

As if she'd been waiting for them to talk about her, Warren heard the clatter of Sophia's claws across the wood floor in the hall. The dog entered the drawing room and sank onto the carpet between the two women. She didn't beg. She didn't whine. She settled onto the floor and went back to sleep.

"I'm…I'm amazed," gasped Warren.

"Eleanor took things in hand with the dog after you left. The veterinarian is please with her progress in such a short time. He thinks we've added years to her life."

Warren finished his cake. Fatigue washed over him in waves. The thought of waves made him feel sick again. He sipped his tea, which helped.

"I'm sorry, Aunt, but I'm going to have to plead exhaustion and not join you for dinner this evening."

"I thought you might feel that way. We planned a light meal for you, but if it's too much, feel free to rest all you want."

Warren swigged the rest of his tea and stood. "Thank you. The cake was excellent, as always. I'll see you ladies in the morning."

"We're planning to dine at Parker's tomorrow for luncheon, if you care to join us," said Aunt Louellen.

Warren stopped and gripped the doorway. He would wake in the morning and find it was all a strange dream. She would be the same old cranky woman she always was, with her passive digs and layer after layer of guilt heaped on him for abandoning her.

"That sounds wonderful, Aunt. I haven't eaten there in a long time."

"Do you need help with anything, Mr. Burke?" Nellie touched his elbow. He turned and found compassion in her eyes and written on her face. "Can we send up a bowl of the soup Cook made for supper? You might need more than cake if you want to rest well tonight."

Warren found himself nodding agreement. "I suppose so. That might be nice. Thank you."

"We'll send it up with Reynolds once you've had a chance to settle from your trip."

Warren shut himself into his room with his trunks. He'd seen other men on trips like his who seemed to travel with an entire household of goods in their luggage. He tried to fit everything into two trunks. He removed the items and placed them in his drawers. He knew Reynolds would do it if he asked, but Aunt Louellen kept the poor man hopping.

For the first time ever, Warren considered he hadn't brought anything back for his aunt. Or Nellie. Why had he never thought to do so before? His uncle had always brought things back for those at home. So had his father. He made a mental note to change this habit. He'd grown so accustomed to traveling to and from meetings with vendors, choosing what he wanted and leaving the rest, eating in his favorite restaurants. Going straight from his room, to the restaurant, to his office and back again at the end of the day. If his aunt could change, so could he.

A tap sounded on the door. Warren found Reynolds outside, holding a tray with a bowl of thick soup. "Cook sent your dinner. She said you might be too tired to wait until later. Madam ordered soup because of the weather. It seemed a fitting meal for someone returning from a long journey."

"Thank you, Reynolds. You can set it on the desk."

"Do you want me to unpack your trunks, sir?"

"I've already finished. You can remove them to the hall closet. I won't be needing them for a while this time."

"Very well, sir." The older man carried the trunks, one at a time, out of the room. He peered in the bedroom door when he'd finished. "Do you need anything else, sir?"

"Not tonight," said Warren. He hesitated. "Reynolds, I'd like to ask you something."

Reynolds entered the room. Warren shut the door behind them.

"My aunt and Miss Greene. Are they getting along or are they putting on an act to keep me from worrying?"

"I've never seen anything like it, sir. They had their tiffs the first day or two but that was all. Miss Eleanor can get Madam to do anything. And I mean anything. They have theater tickets for next week."

Warren had seated himself at his desk and sipped the broth from the soup. He choked on it. "Theater tickets? My aunt is going to the theater?" he said, once he'd stopped coughing enough to talk.

Reynolds hurried from the room and came back with a glass of water. "I'm sorry, sir. Cook asked me to bring the water to you, but I couldn't manage both at the same time." He waited while Warren took a drink before he continued.

"It's not only the theater. They're going to the midsummer's eve ball. Miss Eleanor's aunt and uncle invited Madam to their house for dinner beforehand and the whole party will leave from there. They attended the ladies' aid luncheon a few weeks ago. They've been walking the dog around the neighborhood and down to a park not far from here. They've been eating at Parker's every week. Madam has taken to reading..." the poor man glanced around the room, then cupped a hand at his mouth and whispered "... horror novels. She says they don't frighten her but sometimes I hear her pacing in her room at night after a particularly scary section."

"At night? Have you started sleeping here again?"

"No, sir. Sometimes, you know, it takes longer to finish things before the next day. And Madam goes to bed so early."

"Maybe she's not pacing because she's frightened."

"She never used to pace before. I think they like to scare themselves for the fun of it."

Warren sat back in his chair and stared out the window above the desk. They were getting along. Who knew Nellie would make such a good companion for his aunt? It was a stroke of providence, that's what it was.

"Miss Eleanor has Madam going to church again. She told her if she was going to attend the ladies' aid luncheon, she should attend church so she could keep her eye on the members of the group. Now, I think Madam goes because she enjoys it. They always have a hearty discussion about the sermon over Sunday lunch. I think they argue about it for the sake of having an argument because they always come round and act like nothing happened."

"I'm...I'm flabbergasted."

"You went away for a couple months and came back to a whole new aunt."

"She's gone back to how she was when my uncle was alive. You must remember how she was then, Reynolds. She has always been a hard, stubborn woman who got her own way. But in those days she was more adventuresome."

"True, true. Now, Miss Eleanor always gets *her* way. Yet somehow, she makes Madam feel like it was Madam's idea all along."

Warren burst out laughing. "Yes! I can see that! It's remarkable! She's accomplished things none of the rest of us have been able to do for decades."

"I must see to dinner preparations, sir." Reynolds made his way to the door and opened it. "Oh, and if you aren't too busy, they got a theater ticket for you, as well. They've also included you in their mid-summer's eve ball plans. You are welcome to attend both." He left the room and pulled the door shut behind him.

Chapter Thirteen

Warren woke the next morning to sunlight streaming in his window and the sound of a dog yapping in the hall. He heard Nellie shushing the dog, to no avail. He stretched and sat up. He felt refreshed for the first time in weeks.

He heard a scurrying in the hall. The dog yipped again. Warren got up and opened the door a crack in time to hear the dog yip sharply and fall silent. He thought for a moment she'd smacked the dog but he peeked out and saw Nellie had her hand clamped around the dog's muzzle and was carrying it down the stairs.

Warren knew he'd overslept, based on the amount of light filling his room. He needed to oversee unpacking the shipments of goods he'd sent back. He also wanted meet with his manager to look over the books in his warehouse office.

The ladies were finishing their breakfast when he arrived in the dining room. Aunt Louellen had lost the gaunt appearance that caused him such concern before he left. The dog lounged on a blanket next to the kitchen door and appeared decidedly thinner.

"Dr. Greene told me porridge is better for me for breakfast than all the heavy things we were eating before. Cook is saving a bowl for you in the kitchen. Would you like it with or without cream?"

Reynolds brought the steaming bowl and set it in front of him. Warren accepted the cream from his aunt and poured it over the gray, amorphous glob in his bowl. He was thankful it tasted better than it looked. Just the right balance of salt and sweet and a sprinkle of nutmeg across the top.

"We're going for our morning walk before it gets too hot," continued Aunt Louellen. "Do you care to join us?"

"I might join you another day. I have to meet my manager at the warehouse. I was supposed to be there fifteen minutes ago." Warren ate the thick goop as fast as he could without choking on it.

"Such a lovely day. Too bad you have to spend it indoors."

Warren's eyebrows shot up as he stared at his aunt. He tried to cover his surprise with a smile. "I'm so happy you've come to enjoy the outdoors, Aunt."

"I've always enjoyed the outdoors," she said with a sniff, and looked down her nose at him. Some things hadn't changed at all. "The cold bothers me. I had to wait for it to get warmer before I could get out in it."

Warren wasn't going to argue with her.

"There's a lovely little park up the road. One of those green spaces, or community gardens they've been putting in all over the neighborhoods. Aunt Louellen and I like to wander in there on nice days." Nellie smiled at his aunt.

"I guess I can spare a few more minutes to see the garden," said Warren. "I'll phone Mr. Baker and tell him I'm still coming, albeit later than expected." He finished the last of his porridge and stood from the table. "Excuse me ladies."

Warren was waiting for Baker to answer the phone at the warehouse when he realized Nellie's smile had been all it took for him to change his mind about the morning walk. He groaned inwardly but knew there was no way for him to back out now.

The ladies were waiting for him when he finished and arrived in the hall. His aunt took his arm, while Nellie managed Sophia's leash. The dog pranced in circles by the door, eager to be off. She sprang down the steps. With a gentle tug, Nellie brought Sophia to heel next to her. The two set off briskly down the walk, with Warren and his aunt following more slowly.

"You two seem to be getting along fine," Warren said, addressing the thing he'd been concerned about for weeks.

"She's a breath of fresh air around here. I'd forgotten what fun it was to be young and do things. She isn't extravagant. I suppose I have been living more extravagantly than I did for years, though. Have you heard from the solicitor about it?"

"Not a word." Warren didn't tell her about his conversation with Reynolds the previous evening.

"She's been reading to me, you know. Most of the books we've chosen from the library. I had no idea Theodore enjoyed darker books. We've read a few — *Dr. Jekyll and Mr. Hyde*, *Frankenstein's Monster*, *The House of Seven Gables*. I couldn't walk to the park without an umbrella for days after we read *The Raven*. I knew all the birds were watching me and plotting my doom."

Warren chuckled, and his aunt joined him, a sound he hadn't heard since his uncle passed. His laughter died on his lips at the reminder.

"We have theater tickets next week. First, we'll eat dinner at Parker House. Then we'll attend the play. It's a new one Eleanor read about in the paper. I'm afraid it's going to be vulgar. If it is, I'll take a nap until it's over."

Warren laughed again. He couldn't remember his aunt being so pragmatic and found it refreshing.

"I can't see what's funny about it," she said with a sniff. "I feel like it would be a waste of money to attend a play and sleep through it."

"We'll have to trust Nellie did her research."

"Eleanor. She's a lady. Use her Christian name."

"I doubt the play will be that bad, Aunt. I'm happy to see you getting out and enjoying yourself again."

"We haven't been to Parker's for dinner since Theodore died. I can't remember the last time I went to the theater. It all seemed such a waste after he was no longer there to enjoy it with me. Though he never enjoyed the theater. He tolerated going because I enjoyed it."

Warren remembered that about his uncle. They'd all attend together and Uncle Theodore would mock the play under his breath the whole time. Young Warren had connived to sit next to his uncle every time.

They'd reached the park. Nellie had let Sophia off the leash and the little dog tore through the mud puddles left over from the previous day's rain with glee. Her white coat was covered in grime.

Aunt Louellen patted his arm. "Don't worry about Sophia. We always bathe her when we get back to the house. She loves playing in the mud like this. We let her so she'll be better behaved later in the day."

Warren watched Nellie's lithe figure follow Sophia. She never left the trail. Now and then the dog would come barreling back to Nellie, who would laugh and shoo it away. They rounded the bend and began the return trip. Nellie leaned to put the lead on Sophia's collar. The dog shook and splattered dirty water all over Nellie, who screeched then burst out laughing. Warren joined in the laughter and hurried over to offer his handkerchief. Her face and dress were splattered with mud.

Nellie accepted the handkerchief. She was still laughing. "I hope the mud will come out of my dress. Crazy dog! But I should have known she would shake the water off. Look at you, naughty doggy! You're a mess!" She wiped her hands and face with the cloth Warren had given her. "Did I get everything?"

Warren inspected her upturned face. She had a smudge under her eye and another across her nose. He took the handkerchief from her and wiped the smudge away. Then he gently brushed the dirt off her nose. His fingertips grazed her skin. Her silky smooth skin. That flushed under his touch. He handed the cloth back to her. "I think I got it."

Nellie took a step away from him. "Thank you." She sounded out of breath. She started to offer him the handkerchief back then stopped.

Warren stared at the soggy, grimy cloth and held up a hand to refuse it. "I'll get another when I get back. You keep it in case you need it again."

"I need more than a handkerchief, I think," said Nellie. She attempted, again, to wipe the grime off her hands with little success. "I'll make sure this gets laundered and get it back to you. Oh!" Sophia tugged on the lead and Nellie's laugh tinkled through the morning air. "Heel, Sophia. We're going home now."

"She's a lovely young woman, isn't she?" said Aunt Louellen on the walk home.

Warren cut a questioning glance at his aunt, but she looked as if she was stating fact, not trying to convince him one way or other. "Yes, she is. Even when her face is covered in dirt."

Nellie scrubbed the handkerchief in the laundry room. She'd covered the cloth in soap and let it soak all morning. Most of the dirt had come out but two or three spots remained. She'd applied more soap and was working to get them out.

Too late, she noticed a tiny hole had formed where she scrubbed. In horror, she held up the monogrammed handkerchief and saw another, larger hole near the first. She dropped it in the sink and covered her mouth with both hands. What was she going to do? She should have left it for the laundress when she came later in the week. But she'd wanted to prove to herself and Mr. Burke she could do something other than sitting with an old woman day in and day out. Obviously, that 'something other' was not laundry.

She rinsed the soap out and held it up once more. The holes were still there, and had grown from what they were before. She clutched the handkerchief to her chest and tried to think of a way to fix it. She couldn't mend it or patch it. The only thing to do was pay for another.

She groaned and brought the handkerchief up to her face. Despite all the soap and scrubbing, it still smelled like Mr. Burke's cologne. She inhaled the scent, then stopped herself. She was falling back into her old behavior. Mr. Burke was her employer, nothing more. True, he was handsome and kind, the sort of man she'd always hoped to marry.

The old Nellie would have kept the handkerchief. She would have bought another and given it to him instead without ever confessing what she'd done. But the new Nellie forced those notions to the back of her mind. She would not allow them to become the focus of what she said and did in this house. She had a job to do and that job didn't include imagining she was in love with her employer and searching for ways to entrap him.

She carried the handkerchief up to her room and spread it out to dry. Her mind wandered to that morning in the park. How he'd offered his help so quickly, how his fingertips had grazed her skin.

Nellie winced and gave herself a mental shake. She'd done this to herself before. She remembered back to Gran's warning she was imagining interest from Dr. Coburg that wasn't there. She remembered her cousin Meg's rebuke. She had to learn so she didn't repeat it a third time.

But, for a moment, she allowed herself to remember Mr. Burke's warm brown eyes inspecting her face and his gentle fingers brushing off the dirt. Just for a moment, she let herself imagine what it would be like to have the most handsome, eligible bachelor in Boston take an interest in her, a little nobody from a small town in Maine.

Sophia's bark brought Nellie back to reality. She heard Reynolds open the kitchen door to let the dog into the garden. She stared at her reflection in the mirror. She reminded herself she wasn't that girl anymore. She was a woman. A woman who needed to focus on her responsibilities and not on attracting a man. A woman who was responsible for the needs of someone else now.

But she needed to do something about that handkerchief.

They'd finished dinner and Aunt Louellen had gone to bed before Nellie worked up the courage to show Mr. Burke what she'd done to his handkerchief. Part of her wondered if she'd get off easier if she turned on the tears and appealed to his sympathy. The method had worked in the past. But that was another time and she was a different person then, she reminded herself yet again. She took a deep, bracing breath, pulled the handkerchief from her pocket, and knocked on the study door.

"Come in," came Mr. Burke's response.

Nellie pushed open the door. Mr. Burke was reading in one of the leather wing-back chairs near the fireplace.

"How can I help you, Miss Greene?"

"I was hoping you could forgive me, and tell me where I could find another of these." Nellie held up the handkerchief so Mr. Burke could see it in all its holey glory. She watched amusement flicker across his face, though he was too polite to ask outright what she'd done. "I thought I could clean it for you and return it this evening. Sort of a grand gesture in return for the one you did for me earlier when you offered it in the first place. I should have left it for the laundress. I scrubbed holes in it."

His brown eyes held laughter and he'd covered his mouth with his hand, attempting to appear he was deep in thought. Nellie could tell he was trying to hide his amusement and not succeeding. She frowned at him, annoyed. She'd expected anger, not amusement. His laughter wounded her pride. "I never claimed to be gifted in the domestic arts, Mr. Burke. I didn't know it was a requirement."

Mr. Burke laughed out loud. He slapped his knee. "It isn't a requirement, Miss Greene and I appreciate the attempt." He continued to chuckle and pulled out a fresh handkerchief to wipe his eyes. After a moment of effort, he schooled his features. "Please, don't worry about it. I'm sure the same could happen to the best of us." And he was off into gales of laughter again.

"I can't see what's funny about this, Mr. Burke. It was an accident, I assure you."

"I believe you, Miss Greene. Years ago, my mother sent me away to college with enough shirts to last me until I could visit home and get them laundered here. But I was determined to make my own way and that included, I thought, dealing with cleaning my own shirts. I got another fellow in my house to show me what to do. Unbeknownst to me, he knew as little about laundry as I did. I had to wear shirts with holes for a few weeks until I could get home and get them both laundered and repaired."

Nellie's eyes widened as she listened to the story. Then she laughed along with him. "That does make me feel better, but only a little. Women are expected to know about these things. Clearly, that is not the case with me."

Mr. Burke leaned forward and accepted the handkerchief from her. Nellie felt a twinge of disappointment as it left her hand. She'd secretly allowed herself to hope he'd let her keep it.

"Let's hope you are never in a position where you must rely on your own laundry abilities," said Mr. Burke still chuckling. "Please, sit. There's no sense in me sitting in a room by myself every evening while I'm here."

Nellie sank into the wing-back chair opposite Mr. Burke's.

"I owe you my gratitude," Mr. Burke continued. "The difference in my aunt between when I left a couple months ago and now is, well, remarkable. I could almost go so far as to say miraculous."

"Your aunt is a lovely person. I've enjoyed getting to know her. I think she spent too much time on her own. She needed to get back into the company of others."

"I agree. But that is a feat no other person has been able to accomplish." Mr. Burke fell silent. He stared at his book. Nellie thought he'd gone back to reading. "How is your father?" he asked after a moment.

"He's well. He is back in Maine with my mother for a time. He's hoping she'll have everything in order so he can bring her to live here."

“Your mother is living in Maine?”

“No. Well, sort of. My father’s practice was there in a small town. He closed it and moved down here during the epidemic. Afterward, he took over my grandfather’s practice here in Boston. My mother has been closing their house and her mother’s house and overseeing the sale of both properties. It’s taken her some time to do it. My father travels there as often as he can. It’s difficult for a doctor to take time away from his patients.” Nellie hesitated before asking her next question. “What about your parents?”

Mr. Burke stared into the cold fireplace. “My parents have been…gone… for several years now. My mother died when I was a young man, not long after I’d graduated from college. My father died soon after she did and left me in charge of his business. I’d been working with him since college so knew what was expected of me.”

“I’m sorry.” Nellie hesitated. “You’ve been just as alone as your aunt.”

“I supposed I have.” Mr. Burke’s smile was grim. “My responsibilities have allowed me to travel the world. I’m grateful for the opportunity.”

“I’ve always dreamed of traveling,” said Nellie. She felt bad for the morose turn the conversation had taken and she wanted to lighten it. “I thought coming to Boston from my small town in Maine would help, but it hasn’t.”

“There is something to be said for small town life.”

“It’s backward there. Everyone is in everyone else’s business. You have no privacy at all. I never enjoyed it.” Nellie wrinkled up her nose at the memories.

"As if you have much more privacy here. That's one of my aunt's favorite complaints about people here in Boston. She hates being the subject of gossip."

"They *are* brutal. I don't know what I would have done if your aunt hadn't faced some of the people who were gossiping about me."

Mr. Burke raised his eyebrows in question but said nothing.

"We ended up sitting with the worst of them at the ladies' aid luncheon. Aunt Louellen thinks the organizers did it on purpose but we can never prove it. She forced them to talk to me about what they'd been saying behind my back and gave me the chance to answer the accusations. She's got nerve, I'll give her that."

"She's never been worried about what people think of her."

Nellie shifted in her chair. "I need to care for Sophia once more this evening. I've enjoyed our conversation, Mr. Burke." Nellie stood.

Mr. Burke stood as well. "I've enjoyed it. Thank you for joining me. Oh, and thank you for laundering my handkerchief." His eye twinkled at her as he held up the object in question.

Nellie stifled a groan and hurried from the room. She went in search of Sophia. Once she'd found her, she let the little dog out into the garden and waited for her to return. She thought back over her conversation with Mr. Burke. She found it easy to talk to him, though the entire conversation hadn't been deep. Was she shallow, because she couldn't have a conversation with a man that went any deeper than family history and places you'd visited? She didn't know him well. Maybe she needed to get to know him better.

And if she was completely honest with herself, she found him intimidating. Sometimes his eyes got a dark, faraway, mysterious look and she wondered where his mind had wandered. Nellie laughed at herself as Sophia darted into the kitchen. She grabbed the dog and wiped her feet before letting her into the house. Nellie decided she needed to read a different kind of novel to Aunt Louellen. Something without a dark, handsome, brooding man for the love interest.

Chapter Fourteen

The Parker House was dazzling in the evening. Marble gleamed, reflecting back the sparkling light from crystals. Nellie tried hard not to gape as the maitre'd led them on their winding way through the dining room to their table.

Once seated, Nellie gave the menu a cursory glance and set it aside.

"Aren't you planning on eating this evening?" asked Mr. Burke.

"She never orders for herself. She allows me to order for her, trusting I won't get her something disgusting, like monkey brains," said Aunt Louellen with a disdainful sniff.

"Why don't you choose for yourself?" Mr. Burke asked.

Nellie opened her mouth to answer, but Aunt Louellen spoke first. Nellie frowned at her.

"She refuses to learn French. We spent a month working on the fundamentals and she simply couldn't comprehend any of it."

"That's not fair, Aunt Louellen," said Nellie. "I'll admit I didn't try very hard. But we didn't work on it long."

"There are several good French grammars in the study," said Mr. Burke. "You could study any of them at your leisure. And you hardly need to know French to order here. All the waiters use English."

Nellie glared at Aunt Louellen, who stared at her menu and refused to meet anyone's eyes. "I didn't realize that. Aunt Louellen has been ordering in French since we've been coming, so I thought you could only order in French."

"Of course she has. Did they bring you the correct dishes, Aunt?"

"They did get it wrong once or twice."

"See, Miss Greene, even the wait staff doesn't know French." Mr. Burke chuckled and nudged his aunt's elbow.

Aunt Louellen finally met her nephew's gaze. Her haughty expression melted into a smile and she chuckled with him. "I certainly have the pretentious bit down well, don't I?"

Nellie laughed with them. She picked up her menu once more.

Mr. Burke pointed out several important words. "This is *bread*. That word is *chicken*. That one is *sauce*. You'll need to know what kind of sauce, of course. Then you can watch for these words to tell you how the food is cooked." He pointed to several and explained what they meant.

Nellie chose a dish from the menu with Mr. Burke's help. Then she listened as he ordered for the two ladies and made note of how he said the words.

"It doesn't sound that way in my head when I read the words written on the page," she said.

"Ah, yes. The pronunciation will be difficult without a native speaker teaching you."

"I'm not a native speaker, but I know how to say the words," said Aunt Louellen. "I'm willing to help if you decide you want to apply yourself."

Nellie lifted her chin and sniffed in a gesture not dissimilar to the one Aunt Louellen used regularly. "I'd love to learn it, if you will be gracious and not expect me to know everything all at the beginning, and if you'll be patient when I make mistakes."

Aunt Louellen stared at her, then burst out in her rusty, dry laugh. "I'll make a valiant attempt. I suspect we'll both need to exercise patience."

"You do realize the play we have tickets for tonight is entirely in French."

Nellie's eyes flew to Mr. Burke. "You're kidding, right?"

"I'm afraid not. It's a French play. Very popular right now, though I've never seen it. It's more vulgar than Aunt Louellen will like, but it is French." He shrugged.

"I had no idea!" Nellie was horrified. "I mean, I knew it was originally from France. But I thought they'd translated it." She groaned and leaned her forehead onto the palm of her hand. "You'll both be able to understand it and I'll be completely lost."

Aunt Louellen reached across the table and patted Nellie's hand, sympathetically. "I probably won't even be able to stay awake for the whole thing. It's already past my bedtime."

Nellie grinned at the old lady.

"I'm sure we'll find a way to make it so you can understand as well," said Mr. Burke.

"I'd appreciate that," said Nellie.

"Next time we go to the theater, we should make sure it's in English ahead of time," said Aunt Louellen.

Nellie and Mr. Burke laughed their agreement.

∞

The theater was also ablaze with lights and crystal. Mr. Burke helped both ladies out of the car and then escorted them inside, one on each arm. An usher inspected their tickets and led them to their seats — a box on the second floor. They ascended the sweeping staircase, their shoes making no noise in the plush, red carpet.

They seated themselves so they could all see the stage. Mr. Burke sat next to Nellie. Aunt Louellen sat behind them with the opera glasses. Nellie scanned the playbill and fiddled with her gloves and dress. Finally, the lights dimmed and the curtain went up.

Nellie was thankful for the darkness and the beams of light on the stage. For the first time this evening, she could revel in the misery she felt. She'd made a terrible mistake with this play. She wouldn't be able to understand a word of it and the playbill didn't contain a translation. Aunt Louellen would be out too late and might get sick. Reynolds would be annoyed. They'd be back so late he would have to spend the night. Mr. Burke hated social events. She was sure he'd only come to be polite.

Beautiful music swelled from the orchestra pit as the spotlights focused on a young woman striding across the stage. She began to sing.

Suddenly, Mr. Burke's voice, soft, gentle, close to Nellie's ear, explained what the girl was singing. Now Nellie was thankful for the darkness for another reason. It concealed the intimacy of the situation from prying eyes and gossiping tongues. It also concealed the flush that crept up her neck and face. But she didn't move away. In a moment, she was enthralled with the story and hardly noticed it was Mr. Burke's voice giving it meaning.

Warren had determined he'd translate the play for Nellie as soon as he realized she was the only one who wouldn't be able to understand it. He was careful to arrange the seating so he'd be next to her in their box. He hadn't anticipated how close proximity to her would affect him.

She looked lovely tonight. Her golden curls were drawn back on the sides and spilled over her shoulder. She wore a rose dress that made the blue of her eyes stand out. He'd never noticed things like this about women. Yes, they wore dresses and styled their hair. He could see little difference between one style or color and another. He didn't care enough to notice.

But now he did care for some reason. He'd found himself caring more and more over the last days. They'd taken the dog on walks, talked in his study after Aunt Louellen went to bed, discussed newspaper articles over breakfast in the morning. He'd taken both ladies to his warehouse. An unacknowledged part of him had been pleased when Nellie exclaimed over the items that were also his favorite.

He leaned closer and murmured the play's translation into her ear, taking in the expression on her face. She was engrossed in the story unfolding before them and he had a small part in making it happen.

∞

They were long past Aunt Louellen's bedtime when they arrived home. The old lady had fallen asleep in the car. Nellie woke her with a soft, "Auntie, we're home. You need to wake up so you can sleep properly in bed. Let me help you."

Warren helped Nellie with Aunt Louellen. She leaned on them until she was safely in her room, where Nellie shooed Warren out and helped Aunt Louellen prepare for bed.

Warren waited in his study, listening for Nellie's footsteps in the hall. After what seemed like forever, he heard her leave his aunt's room and shut the door. Dog claws clattered on the wood floor and she reopened the door to let Sophia into the room. Then she turned and saw Warren waiting in the hall.

"I hope we haven't kept you waiting too long, Mr. Burke."

"How is she?" he asked.

"She's already asleep. I told her to sleep as long as she could in the morning. I'm worried she'll get sick but she wanted to attend tonight and it was worth it to get her out of the house."

"Did you enjoy the evening, Miss Greene?" Warren's chest hitched as he asked the question. What if she hadn't? What if his continual whispers had annoyed her?

The flush that covered her face and neck was all the answer he needed. Warren smiled and stepped forward. He offered his hand and she took it. Her hand was small and soft and his large hand swallowed it.

"I had a lovely evening, Mr. Burke. Thank you for making sure I could understand the play. It was wonderful." She smiled up at him. Her eyes sparkled with joy.

Warren stepped closer. His hand tightened around hers, a gentle squeeze, almost involuntary. He lifted her fingers to his lips and brushed a kiss across her knuckles. "I haven't had such a lovely evening in a long time. Maybe ever." He knew he had held her hand as long as was proper, but he didn't want to let it go.

Nellie tore her gaze away first. "I must go. Thank you again." She slid her hand out of his grip and hurried up the stairs.

Warren forced himself to not watch her go, though it went against every fiber in his being. He returned to the study, leaned against the mantle, and stared into the cold fireplace. The image of her brilliant smile and bright, joy-filled eyes was burned into his memory. He'd give just about anything to see that look on her face all day, every day.

Nellie hurried into her room and closed the door behind her. Then she leaned against it and tried to catch her breath. She wasn't supposed to be feeling like this about anyone ever again. She covered her face with her hands. Everything she thought she saw in his eyes, everything she'd felt when he was so close to her, was all in her imagination. All of it. She'd made the mistake of imagining feelings that weren't there. She wasn't going to do it again.

But for one moment, she let herself drift into the daydream that he had meant it. She remembered his hand holding hers, his lips grazing her fingers, his eyes gazing all the way into her soul and seeing that, with a little encouragement, she'd fall in love with him.

A tear slid down Nellie's cheek and she brushed it away with her hand. Things would be easier once he went on his next trip. He'd forget all about her, and she'd have an easier time forgetting him, too.

Chapter Fifteen

Warren's second visit with Nellie's family went better than his first. The night of the mid-summer's eve ball, the three of them ate dinner at her aunt and uncle's house. Nellie's parents were also there. Nellie hugged her mother when they entered the house. Then, Dr. Greene caught his wife's elbow and led her over to meet Warren.

"This is my wife, Elaine," he said.

"Elaine and Eleanor. The names are similar," Warren remarked.

"That could be why she received her nickname," said Dr. Greene. "It was easier to tell the difference when her name was shortened."

"She was such a tiny thing. Eleanor was too big a name for such a tiny girl," said Mrs. Greene. "Then the name stuck."

Warren couldn't imagine Nellie so tiny. Not that she was big now. But he could see how a name from when she was little would carry through to adulthood. "Did she ever try to get you to call her anything else?"

"Maybe when she was thirteen or fourteen," said Mrs. Greene. "It didn't work."

Nellie had been standing to the side, talking with her Aunt Ida. She turned toward them. "It didn't work because I stopped trying so hard to get everyone to change. I didn't mind my nickname anymore."

Warren considered the women standing before him. He'd always wondered if Nellie resembled her mother, because she didn't resemble her father. But she didn't look like either of her parents. Her eyes were shaped like her father's but the color of her mother's. She was built like her mother, but had her father's set to the shoulders and jaw. The golden cloud of curly, blonde hair was what confused him. Her father's was dark and her mother's a much darker blonde, almost brown.

Nellie caught his confused examination. As if she'd read his thoughts, she said, "My mother's hair used to be much lighter, before she had me. She said it darkened when I was a baby."

Mrs. Greene gave a self-conscious pat to her hair and laughed. Nellie caught her mother's hand and pulled it away from her hair with a soft rebuke.

The footman called them to dinner. Dr. Greene took his daughter's hand and tucked it in the crook of his elbow. Warren offered his arm to Mrs. Greene. They went through together.

The ballroom was lit, much as it had been in the spring for the debutante ball. This time Nellie felt more confident.

The dancing had already started. Couples whirled around the floor, making Nellie's head spin. Laughter tinkled through the air. The atmosphere was more light-hearted than the debutante ball. All anyone wanted to do tonight was enjoy themselves.

Nellie hung back from the dance floor. Her father led her mother in a reel around the floor, both laughing like the young people among whom they danced. Mr. Burke watched the dance, his arm supporting his aunt.

"Did you want to dance, Aunt Louellen?" he asked.

"Nothing on earth could compel me to whirl around in circles out there and make a spectacle of myself. No, I'm old. Dancing is for young people. Help me sit over there where I can watch," she said.

Mr. Burke escorted Aunt Louellen to a seat, then rejoined Nellie. They watched the dancers until the music came to an end. The first strains of a waltz filled the air. Nellie watched her father slip his arm around her mother's waist and step into the slower steps of the dance. A movement next to her caught her eye and she glanced down.

Mr. Burke held out his hand to Nellie. "May I have this dance?"

Nellie caught the smile behind his eyes, though his face was serious. She laid her hand in his and he led her onto the floor.

"Your parents seem happy to be together again," said Mr. Burke.

"They always miss each other when they're separated. My dad is glad she's back here for good."

"I'm happy for them."

Nellie's parents floated by behind them. Nellie watched them. She was happy for them, too. But watching them only increased the longing she struggled to keep at bay — the desire to have a husband and possibly children of her own, to have someone look at her like she was the only woman in the world, to have a man search out her company above everyone else's. The desire for children surprised her. She forced her thoughts back to the present.

"This ball seems far less formal than the debutante ball," she said.

"Oh, it's much more relaxed. The debutante ball was far too pretentious this year. All those high society women, old and young, who have decided they are in charge of who is most popular. Then you have all those weak minded men chasing the women who have been chosen for them. I attended, but stayed away from anything to do with dancing."

"You were there?" Nellie was shocked. "I don't think I ever saw you."

"I was playing cards with most of the men in a salon on the other side of the building."

"I wish I could have been playing cards. Though Aunt Louellen would probably say that's too vulgar an activity for a proper young lady." Nellie mimicked Aunt Louellen's haughty tone and earned herself a burst of laughter from Mr. Burke.

Mr. Burke tried to school his features when the couples nearby turned to stare at them but didn't succeed. Nellie ducked her head to hide her own laughter.

"You sounded just like her," Mr. Burke whispered.

"I've heard it often enough. I don't mind, though. She's trying to help." Her eyes twinkled up at him. "I must confess, sometimes I do things to shock her and get her to say it."

Mr. Burke tried to hide his own chuckles. He led them to the edge of the floor and spun Nellie to a stop. The music finished a moment later.

Nellie took a deep breath to get her giggles under control. Then she turned to watch the dance floor. She knew no one would offer to dance with her again, except maybe her father. But her father was leading her mother toward the refreshment table, their heads bent together in conversation.

The first strains of a foxtrot floated through the room. Nellie's eyebrows shot up.

"Do you want to horrify my aunt by dancing the foxtrot with me?" asked Mr. Burke.

Nellie grinned up at him and slid her hand into his. "It would be my pleasure."

He was an amazing dancer. He whirled Nellie in and out of the movements without missing a beat. His brown eyes never left hers. Nellie thought he might be the most handsome man present this evening, with the way his tuxedo fit his broad shoulders perfectly, his long face and firm, square jaw, and the easy, purposeful way he moved. Nellie had seen how austere he could be when she first met him. Now all she could see was the smile in his eyes and the gentle, graceful way he led her through the dance steps.

Nellie was out of breath when they finished. The floor exploded into applause. Then the orchestra picked up the strains of another waltz.

"I need a drink. What about you?" said Mr. Burke. He offered Nellie his arm and led her off the floor to the refreshment table.

Nellie glanced at Aunt Louellen. An old lady had taken the seat next to her and the two women, who both had drinks of their own, were engrossed in conversation. Nellie was glad to see it. Aunt Louellen had been excited about the evening. Several times she'd mentioned old friends she hoped would attend. She'd heard from one of the women who'd promised to be in attendance. This must be her friend. Nellie smiled at their animated conversation. She couldn't tell if they agreed or disagreed, but they were doing it with enthusiasm.

"She seems to be enjoying herself," said Mr. Burke as he handed Nellie a cup of bright red liquid. He nodded toward Aunt Louellen. "I was worried it would be too much for her."

"She's been anticipating it ever since we made plans to come." Nellie took a tentative sip. The sweet juice ran down her throat, a mix of grape and apple juice, and maybe some ginger ale. She hoped it was ginger ale. "Do you wish you were playing cards this evening?"

"Not at all," said Mr. Burke. He smiled at her over the rim of his cup as he took another sip. "I haven't danced at one of these things for years. I'd forgotten what fun I was missing. What about you? More fun or less than the debutante ball?"

"More. Far more," said Nellie without hesitation. "I've already danced as much as I did then."

"What? Why? I find it hard to believe a beautiful woman like you would lack dance partners. In fact, I've been chasing them away all evening."

“How?” asked Nellie, shocked.

“My presence keeps them at bay. But, if you’ll turn your attention to the people around us, that man over there has been following you, and that one has started this way three times and each time given up. I think, if they have no more back bone than that, they should be soundly rejected when they finally do work up the nerve to ask for a dance.”

Nellie burst out laughing, not caring if it was ladylike or not. “I thank you for your protection from spineless young men, Mr. Burke. My father will be grateful for your watchfulness.”

“I care nothing for your honor,” said Mr. Burke with a nonchalant shrug. “It’s too much work to find another companion my aunt likes. My motives are completely mercenary and borne of laziness.”

Nellie laughed again, and this time Mr. Burke joined her. Then he collected her empty cup and set it aside. He held out his hand. “They are beginning another reel. I’ve not tried the dance in years. Care to join me?”

Nellie slipped her hand into his and let him lead her onto the floor. He whirled her through the steps with as much skill as he had done the other dances. Nellie was flushed and breathless when it finished and she beamed up at him. She had never had this much fun at a dance.

Warren wanted to keep Nellie all to himself this evening, but he knew he didn't dare. Other young men worked up the courage to ask her for a dance but Warren didn't want to dance with anyone but her. She fit in his arms perfectly. He could anticipate where her hands and feet would be, where he'd need to place his arm when she spun back into it. The thought came unbidden — she was made for him. He tried to dismiss it, like he'd been trying to dismiss it for days.

The dance finished and Nellie made her way across to where he stood. She pointed to his aunt, still engaged in animated conversation with her friend. "It's getting late. Do we need to take Aunt Louellen home?"

Warren watched his aunt try to stifle a yawn behind her hand. "She looks like she's still enjoying herself." He faced Nellie. "One more dance, then we'll go."

"I'd like that," she said.

He led her onto the floor. Knowing it was the last time he'd hold her like this tonight, he tightened his arm around her waist. Not too much. He didn't want to make gossiping tongues wag. But given he hadn't danced with anyone else; they probably already were. Nellie either didn't notice, or didn't care. She moved with him as if she were part of him.

"Have you enjoyed yourself?" He said it close to her ear.

"Yes. More than I thought I would." She sighed a happy sigh. "Thank you for making it so enjoyable."

"It was a pleasure, I assure you."

They finished the song, then made their way across to Aunt Louellen who was walking toward them, leaning shakily on her cane.

"Are you ready to go, Aunt?" Warren asked. He took his aunt's arm and she leaned heavily on him.

"I was ready an hour ago," she said.

"Really? Because I was watching and you seemed like you were enjoying yourself," said Nellie.

"Not as much as you, missy. Looks like you're turning into a popular young woman." Aunt Louellen gave a contemptuous sniff.

"Aunt Louellen, I know you're tired, but you don't need to be hurtful," said Warren.

"How was I hurtful? I was stating a fact."

"It's okay," said Nellie. She took Aunt Louellen's other arm. "Auntie is correct. I was enjoying myself."

The old lady heaved a huge sigh. "I think I was enjoying myself too much. I don't know if I can make it to the car."

"We'll get you there," said Warren, "even if I have to carry you."

"You wouldn't dare," said Aunt Louellen.

"Wouldn't I? Do you want to find out for sure?"

Aunt Louellen straightened and strode toward the door. The doorman waited with their cloaks. Once they were all safely in the car, Aunt Louellen sagged against Warren's shoulder.

"We've worn you out, Aunt," he said.

"You didn't wear me out. I'm suffering from my own desire to act as though I'm young again." A moment later, her breathing evened out and she was asleep.

Warren stared out the window. He was intensely aware of Nellie's presence on the opposite side of Aunt Louellen and he didn't know what to do with this awareness. Part of him wanted to throw himself into getting to know her, possibly woo her. He could see a future with her at his side. He didn't know her well, but he wanted to change that.

The other part of him wanted to run before it was too late. His life had worked fine the way it was for a long time and it would continue to work for a long time to come.

Or would it? Would his life ever be the same now that he'd met Nellie? Would he ever be able to go back to the way things were before? He didn't know.

"I'll be leaving in the morning," he said into the darkness.

Nellie swung to face him. "You haven't said anything about it before. Must you leave so soon?" She sounded hurt.

"I've been putting the trip off for a couple weeks now. I need to visit a supplier in the south. It won't be a long trip this time." This was at least partly true. The trip could take place any time he wanted. He could have even sent his manager. He'd decided to take the trip during the last few minutes.

"Aunt Louellen told me you rarely stay in town this long. I'm glad you were able to come with us on some of our adventures."

She was trying to sound happy for him, but he could hear the strain in her voice. He cringed. what game was he playing? Would she miss him while he was gone?

"I won't be gone long, less than a week if all goes according to plan."

"We'll look forward to seeing you when you get back."

Warren felt like a heel once he'd closed himself in his room. He knew he wouldn't sleep. He brought a valise out of the closet and packed the few garments he would need in it. He'd told Peters to return with the car in time to catch the earliest train south. Warren didn't want to allow himself time to think. Not yet. But he knew he wouldn't be able to escape his thoughts later.

Chapter Sixteen

Nellie overslept the next morning. She'd intended to be up in time to say goodbye to Mr. Burke. By the time she woke to sunlight streaming across her bed through a crack in the drapes, he was long gone.

She pushed out of the bed and threw the drapes open. Heat radiated off the building next door into her room. Nellie lifted the sash, hoping for a breeze, but pulled the lacy sheers across the opening. She knew it would be hot in her room by afternoon no matter what she did.

Once dressed, she hurried downstairs. Aunt Louellen sat at the dining room table, Sophia in her lap, the morning paper spread before her.

"Good morning," Nellie said in greeting.

Aunt Louellen glanced at the clock on the wall. "Yes it is, but only just." She returned to her paper.

Something was wrong. Aunt Louellen hadn't been this cool or distance since the first few days Nellie had been with her. Nellie stirred cream into her porridge, then regarded the woman seated across from her.

"Did you sleep well, Auntie?" she asked.

"As well as could be expected." Aunt Louellen answered without removing her gaze from what she was reading.

"Did the dog wake you? It's already hot outside. I'll take her for her walk as soon as I finish eating."

"We already walked up the street and back. I'm sure that is sufficient for this weather. We don't want to tax her."

"Of course," Nellie said. She pushed the goop in her bowl around, trying to decide if she was hungry. She knew it would be a while until tea.

Neither of the women said anything while Nellie ate. She set aside her empty bowl and reached for her now cool coffee. "I can tell something has happened and you're upset," she said focusing on Aunt Louellen's face.

The old woman wouldn't meet Nellie's gaze. She lifted the paper in an attempt to keep Nellie from seeing her face.

"What did I do, Aunt Louellen?"

"You didn't *do* anything, *per se*, at least not on your own. It was you and my nephew. What were you thinking last night, behaving in such a manner? Causing all those gossiping tongues to wag again?"

"Those old women need to find more constructive ways to occupy their time," said Nellie.

"What do you expect when Warren refused to dance with anyone but you? And this after years of not even attending balls. It's a well known fact you live here with me and he lives here with me. What do you think they're saying?"

Nellie paled at the insinuation. "This can't be true."

"Of course it's true. I'm always here and Reynolds or one of the servants are always here. You have nothing to be concerned about. Except then you behave as you did last night. Then you give their idle tongues more fodder."

"I did nothing wrong last night. Nothing."

"No, you didn't. I was watching you all evening. But you must be careful in the future. My nephew will leave for Europe again in a couple weeks and things can go back to normal. Meanwhile, maybe you should visit your parents for a few days."

The ache in Nellie's chest grew. She felt like a weight was sitting there, making breathing difficult. She knew Aunt Louellen was right. People had already been talking about her. Apparently she was doomed to be under the specter of gossip the rest of her life.

"Mr. Burke left this morning early," Nellie said.

"Oh he did? That's unexpected." Aunt Louellen looked genuinely surprised. "When did you find out he was going?"

"He told us in the car on the way home last night, remember?"

Aunt Louellen considered. "I vaguely remember him mentioning something about a trip."

"I don't know when he left, but he said he was taking the first train out this morning. He said he had to visit a supplier in the south and would be back in a few days."

Reynolds entered the room and was clearing away the dishes. "I don't think he slept at all last night, Madam. He retained Peters all night and left before dawn this morning. I didn't see him before he left, but Peters informed me."

Nellie laid her napkin on the table and stood. “I’m going for a walk. I don’t care if it’s hot out there. I need to get out of the house.”

“I hope I haven’t upset you, my dear. I’m only telling you this for your own good.”

“My own good?” Nellie gave a sardonic laugh. “My own good would be for people to mind their own business and stop making my life and all its boring details part of it.”

She stalked from the room and up the hall. A clatter of claws informed her of Sophia’s approach. “You want to go for another walk, Sophia?” The little dog sat and thumped her tail against the floor as hard as she could. She bounded to Nellie when she saw the leash Nellie had taken from the closet.

Nellie was thankful for the company. She and Sophia walked to the park and walked around and around its trails. She sank onto a bench and stared into the lake at the center of the green space. Weeping Willows bent their branches over the water. The deep shade at the water’s edge, coupled with the light breeze, cooled the air by several degrees. The dog flopped onto the grass at her feet and promptly went to sleep.

She stared across the lake and thought about what Aunt Louellen told her. She knew she had done nothing inappropriate. The previous evening, Mr. Burke had been more attentive than she’d expected. He was her employer. Well, Aunt Louellen was, but he’d hired her. Yet, he’d never left her side all evening. When she’d danced with others, he’d been waiting at the side for her to return. They hadn’t lacked for conversation, either.

He was kind and handsome and funny. He didn't seem to care what others thought or said about him. Nellie wished she didn't care. She'd always cared too much. She thought back to Dr. Coburg and Edward. She'd cared what they thought about her and tried to control how they saw her. But all she'd managed to do was insert herself into those men's lives without regard for how they felt. She'd only been concerned she get married, that she have a man at her side. Deep down, she knew she never would have had the same kind of relationship her parents had with either Dr. Coburg or Edward.

What if the reason Mr. Burke had left was because he'd discovered he didn't want to be around her, either? No. That couldn't be it. He hadn't avoided her the previous evening. They'd escorted Aunt Louellen to her room and Nellie stayed behind to help her prepare for bed. After she'd left Aunt Louellen's room, he'd gripped Nellie's hand and met her eyes. He'd told her he was eager to see her when he returned. She had to believe he'd meant it.

The heat was stifling. Summer had come and brought with it the first real heat wave of the season. Sophia panted in her sleep. Nellie could feel rivulets of sweat running down her back. Even the light breeze was hot. She sighed and stood to walk home. Sophia joined her reluctantly.

As Nellie walked home, she thought back to the summers she'd spent up in Maine. It was hot there, but on the worst days, they'd go to the ocean for a swim and cool down. An idea dawned on her. She and Aunt Louellen could go to Maine for the duration of the summer. Her parents hadn't sold their house yet. It sat furnished, but empty. Nellie hadn't been back there for a couple years.

The idea filled her with excitement. It would get them out of the hot city. They could hire someone local to cook and clean for them. The dog would love it. She bounded into the house in much better spirits than she had been when she left.

She found Aunt Louellen in the drawing room, glowering at the crossword puzzle in the paper. Nellie knew the old woman preferred her help to do them. The heat had put them all in a foul mood.

"I see the walk improved your outlook on life," Aunt Louellen grumbled. "Now, come here and help me with this."

"I've had the most wonderful idea, Auntie," said Nellie, ignoring the old woman's request. "It would get you away from all this heat for the summer."

"You want to go away to the shore, don't you? Well, that isn't an option for me anymore. I sold my property there years ago. No sense having it if I wasn't using it."

"No! That isn't it. I was thinking we could spend the summer up in Maine. My parents still own their house. We could rent it from them for the summer at very little expense. Then, if we decided we wanted to visit the beach, we still could. There's a beach not far from Hollis. What do you think?"

"I haven't left Boston for decades and I don't intend to start now," Aunt Louellen said. "You want to leave so you don't have to face anyone."

Nellie's enthusiasm evaporated into anger. "I want to leave because I'm hot and I know if I go up there, I won't be hot anymore."

"The heat won't last. You'll see. It's not going to stay hot long enough to make the inconvenience of travel worth our while. Now, I'm going to my room until it's time for tea and I don't wish to be disturbed."

Nellie watched her go, then slipped into the dark, cool study for a book. The dog followed and stretched out on the cool stone flagging in front of the fireplace. Nellie decided she'd wait for Mr. Burke to return and share her idea with him. If he agreed, maybe the two of them would be able to talk Aunt Louellen into a trip north.

Chapter Seventeen

Warren jerked awake. The train's rocking had slowed and the brakes were squealing. Again. They must have come to another stop. He kicked himself again for staying up all the previous night. Somewhere along the way, he'd gotten too old to do things like that. He pushed himself into a seated position and rubbed his face with his hands.

A porter tapped on the window of his first class room. He slid the door open when Warren waved for him to come. "They're serving lunch in the dining car, sir."

"Thank you," said Warren and watched the man leave. He wasn't hungry, but he'd missed breakfast and knew he shouldn't wait for dinner. He washed his face at the tap in the corner of the room, then made his way through to the dining car where he picked at the food they brought him.

He tried to tamp down the feeling of guilt that had been plaguing him since he left. He shouldn't have run out like he had. He hadn't needed to make this trip. His manager had sounded shocked when Warren called him from a train station when he'd had to switch trains earlier in the morning. The manager had already had plans in place to make the trip himself.

Warren knew he was running. He was running from his aunt. He'd stayed longer this time, but they always irritated each other the longer they were together. He was running from the city and its inhabitants who were members of his social circles. He barely tolerated them on a good day and he knew he'd overstayed his ability to cope.

But he was really running from Nellie. Not from her, exactly, but from the way she affected him. Unfortunately, he'd forgotten he was bringing those effects with him. The distance hadn't helped him one bit. It had made it worse. Then there was the guilt of leaving her without an explanation. All he'd given was a promise to return in a few days. He hoped he'd have his emotions sorted by then.

Once back in his cabin, he sank into the plush seat and stared out the window at the landscape rolling past. He preferred train travel to any other method. The view had a hypnotic affect on him. He was soon lost in his thoughts.

He'd not known what to expect when he returned to Boston a few weeks earlier. He'd remembered Nellie's sharp wit and tongue and her stubborn adherence to her own preferences. He'd admired those things about her when he watched her stand up to his aunt. Of anyone he'd encountered, she seemed best suited to handle his aunt's capricious moods.

Now, weeks later he found himself replaying conversations they'd had again and again. He found himself searching for ways to make her smile at him, or even better, laugh. She'd asked him about his business one evening at dinner. He'd explained it to her simply. Then she'd asked question after question about it the rest of the meal. She'd comprehended what he did better in one meal than his aunt had in decades of exposure to it. He could imagine Nellie would be shrewd on the sales floor, given the chance, a quality he admired in anyone, but especially in her.

He'd been planning to spend the previous evening at cards with his associates. Then he'd seen the longing in her eyes as she stared at the dancers and he'd known he would dance with her at least once. What folly that had been! To think he'd be happy with one dance.

Warren stood and paced the small cabin. He was falling in love with her. He'd never been in love before. He'd never met a woman he wanted to fall in love with. Until now.

Did he want to fall in love? Did he want the encumbrance that came with a wife and family? If he answered honestly, he wasn't sure. Yes, he desired to pursue marriage with Nellie. But he didn't know if he wanted to worry about her when he was away.

She could always travel with him. He didn't know if she wanted to travel. She'd mentioned her desire to see new places once, but they hadn't talked about it since. She seemed to like being in Boston and preferred it to other places she'd lived. She'd even said she didn't like the small town where she'd grown up. Yet, there was an adventuresome side of her, a willingness to try new things. He suspected she'd love the opportunity to travel the world.

The train whistle announced their arrival in another town. It was soon followed by the sound of squealing brakes. Warren lurched back into his seat.

All he could do was wait, get to know her, ask her some of these questions. But he'd need to find another place to live while he was in town. He knew his performance the previous evening had probably opened them, but especially her, up to gossip. He'd remedy the problem when he got back to town.

He leaned back in his chair once more and his eyes slid closed. Now that he'd given himself permission to analyze his own thoughts and feelings, the guilt had lifted. He began to feel drowsy. He stretched out on his bench and closed his eyes. He'd get a couple hours sleep before the train arrived. Then he'd see to his business and get back as soon as possible. An unexpected thrill of excitement coursed through him at the thought of getting back to his aunt — but especially Nellie — in Boston.

Chapter Eighteen

The heat lingered longer than Aunt Louellen said it would. The old lady was grumpy and out of sorts. Nellie forced her to drink water, not just hot tea or lemonade. She encouraged the cook to fix light, cool foods. She helped Aunt Louellen take a cool bath in the evenings. It did little good. There was no breeze to stir the stifling heat. The morning of the fourth day, Aunt Louellen couldn't even get out of bed.

Nellie called her father, who came as soon as he got the call.

"I'm afraid she is unable to manage the heat well at her age. It's common for the very young and the elderly to struggle," he explained to Nellie once he'd examined Aunt Louellen. The old woman had sent him from the room and refused to hear what he had to say.

"What can I do?"

"There's nothing you can do except try to keep her cool. But it appears you're doing the best you can."

"I thought about trying to get her out of the city, somewhere cooler, and if not cooler during the day, then certainly at night."

"That would be a good idea, if you can talk her into it. I suggested it to Mrs. McGowen but she said she didn't want to leave."

"What about our house up in Hollis?" Nellie asked her father. "It's sitting there empty. Mrs. McGowen could rent it during the summer months. It's cooler there. It's closer to the ocean. We could stay there until it cools down here."

"It's not a bad idea. Your mother is always worrying something will happen to it and we won't be there to take care of it. Let me talk with her and see if she is open to the idea." He patted his daughter's hand. "I think she will be, though. You've got the bigger job of convincing Mrs. McGowen to go."

"Leave that to me," said Nellie. She didn't know how she'd be able to talk the stubborn old woman into it, but she had to try.

Mr. Burke entered the house as her father made preparation to leave. Surprise covered his face.

"Is everything alright, Dr. Greene?" he asked

"As well as can be expected, given the heat. Your aunt is old and her body doesn't tolerate it well any more."

"Is it serious?"

"Not at all. But she could use a change of scenery until the hot spell passes. Nellie and I have talked about some ideas. I'll let her share them with you. In the meantime, I must be off. This heat is making many sick."

Nellie saw her father down the walk to his car, then returned to the house.

Mr. Burke had removed his hat and laid it aside. He turned to Nellie. She felt an odd jump in her stomach when their eyes locked. She saw something there she couldn't explain and didn't dare assume what it meant.

"What are these ideas your father mentioned?" Mr. Burke asked.

“I’d like to get Aunt Louellen out of town, preferably to someplace cooler. My parents still have their house in Maine. It would take us several hours by train, then we’d need to hire a car to take us from Walton to Hollis. But the entire trip could be undertaken with little difficulty. We could hire people to cook and wash for us there. The house is furnished. Even if it’s hot there, it cools down nicely at night. It’s near the ocean and the ocean breezes help regulate the temperatures. We could spend time at the beach every day if we wanted. My father is going to ask my mother if we can rent the house for the rest of the summer.”

“It sounds like an excellent idea. What do you need from me?”

“Your aunt refuses to even consider the possibility. She says the heat will break and everything will be fine. Meanwhile, she’s getting weaker and weaker. I can’t force her to make the trip.”

“Why not?” Mr. Burke’s eyes took on a sparkle of amusement. “You’ve been able to get her to do other things these last few months.”

Nellie hadn’t considered this. He was correct. They’d gone to the luncheon, dined out at least once a week, attended a ball and play together, taken daily walks, among other things. Every time, she’d made the plans and then informed Aunt Louellen of them later. The heat must have been affecting her. She’d lost her will to fight. With a sheepish glance at Mr. Burke, she knew this was a battle she should fight, for Aunt Louellen’s sake as well as her own.

“I’ll make arrangements and get Chloe to begin packing her belongings. I have no doubt my mother will agree to it. Maybe Chloe will even want to come with us.”

"Let me know what the summer rent will be and I'll inform her solicitor."

Nellie nodded. She headed up the hall to Aunt Louellen's room, then stopped. She returned to Mr. Burke who hadn't moved.

"I'm sorry. I neglected to ask about your trip or your plans for the rest of the summer. Welcome back." She smiled up at him. "I'm sure Reynolds is already on his way with some refreshments. The study is cool. If you want to wait there, I'll tell Reynolds where you are."

"Will you join me once you've finished what you need to do?"

Nellie's heart skipped at the hope and uncertainty she heard in his voice. "I'd be happy to. I go and sit in there often the last few days. I tried to get Auntie to do it but she said the chairs were too hard."

"Until then," Mr. Burke said.

Nellie flushed and hurried back toward Aunt Louellen's room.

Chloe sat on the edge of the bed with a cloth dipped in cool water. She wrung it out and laid it across Aunt Louellen's forehead.

"Auntie, we're taking a trip. I know you don't want to go, but my father thinks you'll feel better if you get out of town." Nellie brushed her fingers across the old lady's frail arm and took her hand.

Aunt Louellen removed her fingers from Nellie's. "I'm not going. I'm too sick to travel."

"We're going north. It's cooler there, at least in the evenings. It would be a relief for you. There's no sense in you suffering like this. I'm going to make the arrangements for travel in a moment. I wanted to know," she turned to Chloe, "did you want to come with us or should I arrange for a lady's maid there?"

Chloe's eyes lit up. She flicked her gaze from Aunt Louellen to Nellie and back. "I'd…I'd love to go. I didn't think you would ask. Yes! It'll take me some time to make my own arrangements but I'll be ready."

"We won't be going until tomorrow at the earliest," said Nellie. "I can't see how we'd get everything done before then. We might not leave until the day after. But I'll make sure to include you in the train tickets." She beamed at the other young woman and turned to leave.

"I won't go," said Aunt Louellen. "You can't force me."

Nellie stopped with her hand on the doorknob. She took a deep breath before turning to face Aunt Louellen.

"It's for your own good. This heat is killing you, little by little. You're right, I can't force you. But I'm going to make all the arrangements and I'm leaving on the train with Chloe. If you choose not to go, you'll lose the cost of the train ticket and will have to suffer here alone with only Reynolds for company."

The old woman fought to stand. She managed to stay on her feet for a moment or two, before collapsing, exhausted and winded, back on the bed. She sank into the pillows and heaved a sigh. "Alright, you win. I'll go. But if I hate it there, we won't stay long."

"I can agree to those conditions," said Nellie. "I won't force you to stay there if you're miserable. But I don't think you will be. I think you're going to love it."

"If you think I'm going to love it so much, why did you leave?"

Aunt Louellen's barb stung when it hit home. Nellie cringed at the memories flooding back in waves. "I was a foolish, immature, selfish girl. I left because I didn't want to listen to the people who loved me most and had my best interest at heart. My only consolation is if I hadn't left, I wouldn't have met you. Now, I need to go see about some train tickets."

She stepped out of the room and almost into Mr. Burke's arms. The man took a couple steps back as Nellie laughed awkwardly. "Did you overhear everything?"

"I couldn't help it," he admitted with a shrug. "Reynolds was here, but he disappeared into the kitchen as soon as he heard you coming." Mr. Burke winked at her and Nellie laughed again. "Come, we need to talk before you buy those tickets."

Nellie's heart sank as she followed him into the study. "You don't think we should go? I thought you did."

"It's not that. I think you should go. But I'm leaving for an extended trip to Europe in a few days. I've had the tickets for months. There is no sense in leaving the house open. While you were in there, I suggested to Reynolds we close the house until you return in the fall. You'd need to take along everything you need for Aunt Louellen to be comfortable. Reynolds would stay here as caretaker. We'd keep Cook on retainer, unless she agrees to go with you."

"There are women in Hollis who could cook for us. There isn't any reason to uproot us all."

"Then we won't even give Cook the option. I doubt she'd take it anyway. She might be thankful for the break from the hot kitchen."

Mr. Burke sat in the chair near the fireplace and Nellie took her usual seat across from him. She sank into the cool leather and enjoyed the relief from the heat for a few moments before it warmed to her body's temperature.

"I could delay my trip and see you all safely north," Mr. Burke suggested. Nellie thought she detected hope in his voice. She imagined he wanted to get away from this heat as well.

"That won't be necessary. If you've had the tickets for a while, you need to go."

"Then, you must keep in touch. I'm worried about my aunt's health. Is there a doctor in Hollis who can look after her?"

"Dr. Grey has been there for years. He'd like to retire, but no one has come to the town to take his place." Nellie thought back to Dr. Coburg's short tenure there with a twinge of remorse. She'd always feared she'd been the one to chase him away, though Meg always said he was too much a city boy to ever enjoy the country. "My father practiced there but moved here during the epidemic to help my grandpa. He took my grandpa's practice when he retired and moved west a couple years ago."

"Dr. Grey could care for my aunt?"

"Yes, sir. Without any trouble at all. He took wonderful care of my grandma."

"You will write me and keep me up to date on her well-being?"

Nellie's heart thrilled at the prospect of corresponding with Mr. Burke. She tried, and failed, to stop the delighted smile she knew covered her face. "Of course. If it will put your mind at ease."

Mr. Burke leaned back in his chair and heaved a huge sigh of relief. "I cannot express what a relief it will be. I couldn't stop worrying about her through my last trip. I had no idea how the two of you were getting along. I didn't know the state of her health or if it had improved."

"I assure you, sir, if there had been any trouble at all, we would have contacted you immediately. Reynolds surely would have, if I was unable to do so."

"I know. But I still worried." He stood, restless, and paced the room. "A part of me wishes I could take both of you on this trip with me. It's been so many years since Aunt has been to Europe. It's a different place after the war. But I doubt she could make the trip."

Nellie had always wanted to travel in Europe. She'd imagined marrying some rich gentleman and honeymooning there. She had to turn away from Mr. Burke to hide the look of guilt and sadness that passed over her face. He was a rich man who could take her places. But she wasn't about to make the same mistakes she'd made before. She stared at the empty fireplace. "There's no way she could make the trip. I couldn't persuade her to even try. Maine, however, is a bit easier to pull off on such short notice."

Mr. Burke dropped back into the chair across from Nellie. He took both her hands in his own. His thumb traced a path across the back of her hand. Nellie's gaze shot to his. He was searching her face for something. She had no idea what it could be.

"Promise me you'll write often. If not every day, several times a week. I'll leave addresses where you can sent the post."

"I promise to write you," she said. "But you have to write back. I want to hear all about Europe and what you're seeing and doing. Well, as long as it isn't too boring." She chuckled. "You can keep the boring parts to yourself."

He didn't laugh. Instead, he brought both her hands up and pressed them to his lips. She could feel the stubble on his chin.

"I'm going to miss you. I wish you could come with me." His words were soft enough, Nellie didn't know if she'd heard them.

"We'll miss you, too."

"We? Or you?" Mr. Burke stared at her, eyes so intense Nellie felt he was seeing her thoughts and feelings.

Before she could answer, they heard Reynolds coming up the hall. Mr. Burke dropped her hands and stood.

Reynolds entered the open door with a large tray. "Cook sent breakfast for you, sir." He carried the tray to the desk and set it down.

"Thank you, Reynolds."

Nellie stood and crossed to the door. Mr. Burke's voice stopped her.

"Let me know when you've made your travel arrangements. Reynolds and I will make our plans once we know yours."

"I still can't believe she's agreed to this," said Reynolds with a shake of his head. "You can get Madam to do things no one's been able to get her to do for years."

Nellie heaved a sigh. "I suppose it's because she had no other options. This is her only choice. It's not fair, but it works." She turned and went in search of the paper so she could find the train schedule for the next couple days.

Chapter Nineteen

Two days later, the trunks were packed and loaded into the car and everything in the house had been draped with cloths or packed away to protect it against the heat. Sophia made one more visit to the back garden. Nellie hoped all the walking at the station would be enough to tire the little dog out for the train trip.

Her mother was meeting them at the station and would travel to Hollis with them. She'd stay for a few days to help open the house again. Then she'd return to Boston to be with her husband. Nellie looked forward to the time with her mother. She hadn't seen her much the last couple years. Nellie knew that was her own fault. She'd been angry at her parents for making her wait to marry Edward. For a long time, she'd blamed them for what happened. Nellie hoped her mother could see her change of heart.

She made one final pass through the house while Chloe and Reynolds helped Aunt Louellen into the car. She found Mr. Burke at his desk in the study.

"You aren't going to see us off?" she asked. She'd meant it to be teasing, playful, but feared it came out accusatory.

"Maybe I don't like saying goodbye," he said with a small smile. He stood and picked up an envelope from the desk and approached Nellie.

"I can't blame you there. Could we say, like they do in French, *'au revoir'*?"

"I'd prefer that." He stopped in front of Nellie and held out the envelope. "Here are the addresses where I can be reached by post or telegram. Please don't hesitate to use the latter in an emergency."

She took the envelope and tucked it into her handbag.

"Remember, you promised."

Nellie's gaze met Mr. Burke's. There was something there, something she recognized but couldn't name. She smiled at him in an effort to reassure him. "I haven't forgotten. You promised, too."

"You never answered my question the other day."

"Oh? Which question was that?" Nellie couldn't remember him asking her anything.

"Will you miss me?"

He'd stepped closer to her. Nellie's breath hitched around the fluttering in her chest. She couldn't tear her eyes from his. They seemed to bore into her very soul. She tried to take a step back, but found her legs refused to respond.

"Of course I'll miss you. Terribly." She hoped she didn't sound glib. Admitting it was a relief. But the relief was followed immediately by fear. What if…?

Nellie didn't even have time to complete the thought before Mr. Burke's hands cupped her chin and his lips closed over hers, soft, warm, insistent. He broke away, catching a small breath before he pulled her into his arms and kissed her again. Nellie gripped the lapels of his day jacket and kissed him back.

He drew away slowly. His eyes took in her whole face, as though he was memorizing every feature. His hands slid down her arms and he brought her hands to his lips. "I'll miss you with every fiber of my being. Say the word and I'll cancel my trip and come to Maine with you."

Tears filled Nellie's eyes, though she didn't know why she was crying. She blinked them away. "You must go. Your business depends on it. But we'll be here when you get back. Don't worry about us. I'll take good care of Aunt Louellen."

"But who will take care of you?" he breathed, as he brushed her lips with his own.

Nellie knew if she didn't pull away and leave now, she wouldn't be able to. His face was still so close to hers. She pressed her mouth to his one more time, then stepped back. She pulled her hands from his and hurried to the front door. She stopped with her hand on the knob and faced him.

Warren wanted to run after her. He wanted to unload everything from the car and tell them they were making a terrible mistake and needed to stay. Or better yet, insist they come with him to Europe. But he knew Nellie was right. He needed to make his trip and she needed to make hers. He would see her again.

Her smile when she glanced back at him was almost his undoing. He forced himself to stand in the doorway of the study and watch her leave the house. Then he took the stairs to his room two at a time. He would finish his packing right now so he'd be ready to leave in the morning. Anything to keep his mind off the beautiful woman who'd just walked out the door.

∞

The train's gentle rocking lulled Aunt Louellen to sleep. They had the windows open in their carriage. The breeze felt wonderful after the stifling heat of the city. The farther north they went, the cooler the breeze became. Nellie sighed with relief.

Her mother patted her hand and smiled at her. "It's been a busy week for you, hasn't it? If you need to rest, feel free. We'll have time to catch up in Hollis."

Nellie was struggling to keep her eyes open. She smiled at her mom and drifted off to sleep.

The squealing brakes woke her some time later. They'd reached Portland. One more station and they'd need to hire a car to finish the journey.

Sophia whined and scraped at the door, so as soon as they were stopped, Nellie put the dog on the lead and took her out into the grass. She had to admit, it felt good to stretch her legs. The weather here was noticeably cooler than it had been in Boston. Nellie could smell the ocean on the breeze. It smelled cleaner, saltier, here. In Boston, she thought it smelled like rotten fish and stale water. She inhaled deeply again and again, savoring the scent.

Aunt Louellen was awake when she returned to the carriage. Her eyes were brighter and she appeared more alert and rested than she had in days.

"How long have I been asleep?" she asked.

"Several hours," said Elaine. "You look refreshed."

"I feel so much better," Aunt Louellen said. "It's cooler." She tried to stand. Chloe hurried to her aid and helped her out of the carriage so she could walk around. Sophia scampered after them, dragging her lead behind her. Nellie rushed after the dog until she saw Chloe pick up the lead. The little dog darted between their legs. She wanted nothing more than a walk with her mistress.

"This was a fantastic idea," said Elaine. She squeezed her daughter's elbow. "Mrs. McGowen has improved already. I think the next few weeks will do wonders for her health."

"I hope so," said Nellie. "I was worried she wouldn't survive the summer."

"What about her nephew?"

"Oh, he'll be fine. He's leaving for Europe tomorrow. I've never been outside of New England, but I'd imagine it's cooler out on the ocean than it is in the city. Have you ever been to Europe, Mama?"

"Once, years ago. Your father traveled to London for a medical symposium and I went with him. It was before you were born. I'd imagine it's changed since then."

"They have cars instead of horse drawn carriages. Of course it's changed. I'd love to see it sometime. I think I'd love to see anything outside the tiny corner of America I've lived in my whole life. Maybe I should plan to visit Meg and Jack sometime."

"They're planning a visit here once the harvest is finished. I think Meg wants to show off little Levi."

"Why didn't they name him Jack after his dad?"

"They did. It's Jackson Levi. They're calling him by his middle name to make things easier."

The train let out a long whistle. Aunt Louellen and Chloe picked up their pace to make it back to the carriage in time.

"I should have kept in touch with Meg better since Gran died and she got married. I wish I hadn't left things unresolved between us for so long."

"You can still remedy that. I know she'd love to hear from you. She asks after you in every letter she writes. Her letters have been fewer and farther between since the baby came, though. But it sounds like farm life agrees with her."

"She always did enjoy helping Gran in the garden and putting up the vegetables at the end of the year. More than I did anyway. I think I'm a hopeless cause when it comes to the domestic arts."

They helped Aunt Louellen into the carriage and settled her in her seat. A few minutes later, the train lurched forward. Nellie brought out the basket of food Cook had sent with them that morning. They all felt better, hungrier, with the cessation of the heat. Once they'd eaten their fill, Nellie tucked the basket away. Aunt Louellen stared out of the window for several minutes before falling asleep again.

The breeze stirred Nellie's hair. She felt drowsy. But she didn't want to miss the approach to Walton. She wanted to see the familiar scenery. It had been too long since she'd made this trip.

The whistle sounded at a cross street. The late afternoon sun streamed across the sky, but Nellie could see clouds building on the horizon. They'd have a shower this evening that would cool things even further.

She wondered what Mr. Burke was doing. His goodbye replayed in her mind over and over. She could still feel his lips on hers. What if he decided there was someone better for him? She forced the thought from her mind and sat up straighter. She had to stay awake.

The train arrived in Walton. Nellie, Elaine, and Chloe unloaded all their belongings from the carriage. Then, while Elaine made sure they got all their trunks, Nellie went in search of transportation to Hollis. It took her a few minutes to find someone who'd drive them there.

She located a lory to carry their trunks without any trouble. However, she had no idea where to find a car that would be comfortable for Aunt Louellen.

The train station was a couple blocks from the hospital. Nellie wandered toward the hospital, feeling nostalgic. As she turned back to the train station, a familiar figure exited the hospital.

"Dr. Grey!" she called to the elderly doctor who was crossing the road toward his car.

The man stopped and stared at her for a moment before he recognized her. "Nellie Greene?" he called out and hurried toward her. "It's been years. What's brought you back to Walton?"

"I'm companion to an elderly lady who needs a break from Boston's summer heat. We're on our way to stay at my parent's house in Hollis for the rest of the summer."

"I heard they were selling their house. Maybe this way they'll decide to keep it and use it as a summer home." His eyes twinkled at her. "We hate to lose any more members of the community." He hesitated. "How are you getting to Hollis?"

"I've hired a truck to carry our trunks. Now I'm searching for a car to take our persons. Do you know where I can find a car to hire?"

"My dear girl, there is no need whatsoever for you to hire a car. I'm going home now. I'd be happy to take you."

"Thank you, Dr. Grey," Nellie breathed with relief. "You have no idea what a help this is."

"What are neighbors for? Let me take you back to the train station to collect your friends."

Nellie was thankful for the long summer days as the Hollis road carried them in and out of the woods. Now and then the road bordered the ocean. The waves were calm, lazy, as if they knew the weather was too hot to do anything more than slide back and forth. Now and then a particularly energetic wave would splash its white spray onto the rocks. Then the water would return to its lazy rocking.

Dr. Grey and Elaine chatted in the front seat. Nellie and Chloe supported Aunt Louellen in the back seat. Nellie held Sophia in her lap. The dog wanted to hang her head out the open window, but Nellie wouldn't let her.

Hollis hadn't changed in the more than two years since Nellie left. Sure some of the buildings had received a coat of paint. The church had a new sign out front, and by the looks of it, a new pastor. Nellie wondered what had happened to Rev. Norton.

They reached the small group of houses constituting her parent's neighborhood. Lights blazed in all the windows except theirs.

"It's rather small," said Aunt Louellen as they helped her out of the car. "It reminds me of the summer home my parents took me to when I was a child. That place was hardly more than a one room shack. Some of my best memories took place there."

Nellie smiled and linked arms with Aunt Louellen as she escorted her up the walk. "My best memories are in this place."

Elaine hurried ahead and unlocked the door. She hadn't been away long. She ran through the house, uncovering the furniture and lighting the rooms.

"No electricity?" asked Aunt Louellen.

"Not yet," said Nellie. "You won't even miss it."

They thanked Dr. Grey and waved as he drove away. Then they went into the house for the night.

They put sheets on the beds and figured out where everyone would sleep. Aunt Louellen got the master bedroom and Chloe took the room across the hall from her. Nellie planned to sleep in her former bedroom and her mother would share with her while she was there.

Once they'd eaten a light supper of bread Cook had sent with them and preserves Elaine still had in the pantry, they all settled in for the night. Nellie had never been so thankful to stretch out on a bed. Her mother had set up a camp cot they'd used when Nellie was a girl and her friends stayed over.

A light breeze fluttered the curtains on the open window. Nellie heard night noises in the woods — the screech of bats as they hunted, a hooting owl, bramble cracking as a larger animal, maybe a deer, walked past. She missed the city noise, but she didn't miss the heat.

A moment later, all the noise faded as the first patters of raindrops hit the roof. Nellie heaved a contented sigh. Her eyes slid closed and she drifted to sleep, the first real rest she'd had in days.

Chapter Twenty

Morning light streamed in the bedroom window. Nellie squinted and looked at her watch. It wasn't even six-thirty in the morning. She stifled a yawn.

The house was silent. Outside, birds called cheerily to one another. The steady *drip drip drip* of rainwater leftover from the previous night dropped into a collection barrel below.

Nellie pulled the covers up to her chin. She shivered. The morning air was much cooler than she'd expected. She closed her eyes and tried to sleep. In a few minutes, she knew it was a lost cause. She slid out from under the warmth of the covers and dressed as quietly as she could. As she slipped into her shoes, she examined her mother who slept on the camp cot. Elaine never stirred.

Then she slipped down the stairs and into the kitchen, where she grabbed the shopping basket and left the house. Mr. Miller would be opening his shop any time now and they needed food for breakfast.

It wasn't a long walk to Main Street. Nellie reached the boardwalk as Mr. Miller turned his sign from 'closed' to 'open'. The bakery next door to the grocery already had the door propped open. The most delightful smells wafted out. Nellie's stomach rumbled. She drifted into the shop as the smells drifted out.

After long consideration, she chose muffins and cinnamon rolls and danishes. She added a loaf of bread so they'd be able to enjoy the preserves again today. Next door, at Miller's Grocery, she bought coffee, tea, milk, and a small pack of sugar.

Nellie meandered through the sparkling morning. She lifted her face to the sunshine. She'd need to get Aunt Louellen out for a walk before it got warm. But even the hottest part of the day here would feel better than Boston.

Elaine had the teapot bubbling on the stove when Nellie reached home. The two women fixed coffee, and ate one of the sweet treats Nellie had purchased. Chloe joined them as they finished. Sophia romped in the back yard, happy to run and play without a lead.

Still, Aunt Louellen slept on.

Nellie checked on her frequently as the morning wore on. The heat had taken its toll on the old woman. She was resting for the first time in days.

At midday, Aunt Louellen still wasn't awake. Nellie found her mother in the kitchen, slicing bread for lunch.

"Should we get Dr. Grey to come check her?" Nellie asked her mom.

"Only if she's sick when she wakes. She probably needs her sleep. I know I didn't sleep well in Boston. The cool weather last night was a relief. I slept better than I have in weeks."

Nellie chuckled. "I can completely understand. I only wish I could have slept longer." She grew serious.

"We need to make some decisions. For instance, who can we get to help with the cooking and cleaning?"

"Are you sure you don't want to do it?" Elaine's eyes twinkled at her daughter. "It'll give you something to do this summer."

Chloe had wandered into the kitchen in search of food. "I have a feeling we'll all have plenty to do," she said. "Mrs. McGowen is sleeping now, but once she wakes up she'll have all of us hopping."

"You're right," said Nellie. "Mama? Anyone we can hire to help us?"

"What about Mrs. Stuart or her oldest daughter, Emily?

"The Stuarts still live here?" Nellie was surprised.

"Of course. Mr. Stuart is headmaster of the school. I'm sure Mrs. Stuart would be happy for the extra income. We can ask. Maybe she could help with the cooking and Emily could help with the cleaning and wash."

"It's a good idea. We can walk over there and ask in a few minutes. We also need to figure out a better way to grocery shop. Obviously, I'm not the one to go to the store. Especially not when I'm hungry." Nellie waved at the plate of pastries leftover from breakfast.

"We'll all gain a ton while we're here if we let you decide on breakfast every day," said Chloe with a giggle.

"Speak for yourself," said Nellie. "I'd take Mrs. Griffin's cinnamon rolls over porridge any day of the week."

"You know Mrs. McGowen will want her porridge. Doctor's orders," Chloe reminded her.

"I can hear your father giving those orders," said Elaine.

"He told her to eat it because she refused to eat anything. And the dog won't eat the porridge so she wasn't tempted to give it to the dog. I can't blame Sophia." Nellie sighed. She was so tired of porridge. "Maybe we can find a compromise. Porridge some mornings, pastries on other mornings."

"Mrs. Stuart can help you with the shopping. You can work together on the menu and let her shop for it. That would be easiest."

"We'll ask her about that, too. Should we get going?"

Aunt Louellen shuffled into the room, swathed in her dressing gown. Her silvery hair was tumbled about her shoulders. She gave them a sleepy smile. "I had the most heavenly rest last night. Do we have any coffee and porridge? I'm hungry."

Nellie and her mother jumped up to find food for Aunt Louellen. "We don't have porridge, but Mrs. Griffin's bakery had the most wonderful pastries. I thought you might enjoy them for a change," said Nellie, hopeful Aunt Louellen would be open to something different."I don't care what I eat and those smell fabulous. I hope I can sleep like that every night. I haven't felt this rested in weeks."

"We'll have to write Mr. Burke and tell him you rested so well last night," Nellie said. "He was worried about you. He wanted to come with us to make sure you were okay before he left on his trip."

"Silly boy! He needs to go on his trip far worse than I need him here. I hope you told him that."

"I told him he needed to make his trip. I did not call him a silly boy."

∞

Nellie and her mother walked to the Stuarts that afternoon. The warm sun beat down on them, but, despite the heat, Nellie wasn't miserable. It felt good to be home. She found she had missed Hollis.

"Have you been spending a lot of time with Mr. Burke?" her mother asked.

Nellie glanced at her mother, unsure of the motives behind the question. "He's been away on business most of the time I've been living with Aunt Louellen. Why do you ask?"

"He was certainly attentive the night of the ball. I thought he was rather taken with you."

Nellie dismissed her mother's words with a flick of her hand and a frown. "He'd heard how things went at the debutante ball. I think Aunt Louellen made him promise not to let it happen again."

"He didn't strike me as a man being forced to dance with a woman out of a sense of duty. I thought he was enjoying himself."

"Mama, please," said Nellie. A pained expression crossed her face. "He was only being polite. I don't want to assume feelings or intentions that weren't there." She remembered his kisses again. For a moment, she was lost in the memories. Her mother's voice brought her back to the present.

"I don't think you were imagining anything at the ball. Mr. Burke never showed attention to any other woman," said Elaine.

Nellie's eyes got a far away look in them. "You're right, Mama. But I'm afraid of repeating past mistakes."

Elaine placed her hand on her daughter's elbow and drew her to a stop. She faced Nellie. "Don't be so afraid of repeating perceived mistakes from your past that you won't move forward into your future. I had the chance to talk to Mr. Burke at dinner and thought he was a gracious man. Your father speaks highly of him."

"You've talked with Daddy about this? Mama." Nellie's tone held a rebuke. She marched away from her mom, embarrassed.

Elaine caught up with her daughter. "I only asked about him. I wanted to make sure Mr. Burke was honorable if you were going to be staying in the same house with him. Your father enjoys his company and approves of your job as a companion to Mrs. McGowen. That's all he said on the matter."

Nellie didn't feel like discussing this any more. She kept quiet until they reached the Stuart house.

Mrs. Stuart welcomed them with open arms. All her girls were school age now, but they were on holiday for the summer months. The house was bursting with chatter and giggles.

Mrs. Stuart sent the younger girls outside so she could talk with the Greenes. She and Emily settled them at the kitchen table with glasses of tea and cookies, while they worked on dinner preparations.

Nellie explained what they needed — a cook, and someone to do the cleaning and their wash. When she told them what she was offering for pay, Mrs. Stuarts eyes widened and she whirled to face the stove.

"Mama, it would be a big help to have the income this summer."

"I'm aware of that, Emily," Mrs. Stuart said. She faced Nellie and Elaine again. "I'd planned to refuse. I can't neglect my family just to earn extra money. But you've made it almost too good to pass up."

"I didn't want to insult you," Nellie explained. She didn't tell the ladies she was offering far less than they'd earn for the same positions in Boston. She knew they'd turn her down if she offered too much. "We need the help. We can be flexible with your needs. You don't have to cook at our house. You can cook here and bring it over. Or I can come get it from you. We'll be paying for everything. Besides, there's only three of us and we don't eat much."

"One of them can fix breakfast so all you have to cover is lunch and dinner," offered Elaine.

Nellie cut her mother a horrified look. She didn't know if she *could* fix breakfast for them, not if they ate porridge. She'd burn it for sure. No, if she had to cook, she'd be visiting the bakery daily.

"We only need Emily twice a week for a morning or afternoon. It won't be all day," said Nellie.

"I'll do it!" said Emily without hesitation. "I can save the money for teaching school. Mama, I think you should cook for them."

"We can try it for a few days and see if it works out," Nellie offered. She dreaded the possibility of doing everything on her own.

Mrs. Stuart continued to stir the food that no longer needed stirring, lost in thought. She finally laid the spoon aside and took a seat at the table. "Okay. I'll try it for a few days. As it is, I've fixed enough for us here plus extra. I could send some with you for your dinner. Then you can try my cooking and see if you even want it."

Nellie opened her handbag and removed the money she'd set aside for food for the rest of the week. She was worried it wasn't enough until she saw Mrs. Stuart's eyebrows shoot up. "This is for the week," she explained.

"How about I use this until it's gone and let you know when I need more?" Mrs. Stuart suggested.

"I have a food budget laid out that I planned with our cook in Boston. We set aside a certain amount for each week. I want you to have enough."

"Food must cost a lot more there. Let me see how much I need and we can make adjustments."

Nellie agreed and reached down to close her handbag. Inside, she saw the envelope Mr. Burke had given her before they left. He was probably on his boat, sailing away from Boston and the United States. She'd forgotten to find out when he was coming home. She owed him a letter when she got home that night. He'd want to know how the first couple days had gone, even if it took until he reached London to receive it.

Chapter Twenty-one

The sun beat mercilessly on the ocean liner and the water glittered with the light of a thousand diamonds, blinding anyone who made the mistake of staring too long. Warren stood at the railing and watched the wake they left behind. He knew he should be thinking about his trip to England and the Continent. However, he'd left his heart far behind in Maine.

"Mr. Burke," said the steward who'd approached from behind. "You must come out of this hot sun. You'll get sunstroke. Come with me and have something refreshing to drink under the canopy over there." He waved his arm indicating the nearby deck chairs. Warren followed him to the shaded area.

Warren sank into the chair's cushion and accepted the cool water the steward pressed into his hand. He drank it all and held it out to the steward for more.

"We're asking people to be cautious until we get further north," said the steward. "We do have a doctor on board, but, as they say, an ounce of prevention is worth a pound of cure."

The steward moved away. Warren leaned back in the chair. He hadn't tried the chairs on this deck. The one he'd tried earlier in the day hadn't had a flutter of breeze to stir the air. Despite the cool air now flowing over his face, Warren felt sweat trickling down his forehead. He brought his handkerchief up to swab it off and stopped. His finger stuck through a hole rubbed there by Nellie. He'd grabbed the wrong handkerchief.

He fingered the holes and wondered what the women were doing right now. Was it cooler there? Had they gotten settled in the Greene's home? Was Aunt Louellen feeling any better? He hoped there would be post waiting for him in London.

"Mr. Burke!"

Warren sat up straighter and opened his eyes. An old business associate, now a competitor, strode toward him, looking cool and fresh. Warren wanted to hate him, but couldn't.

"How are you my friend?" the man asked.

"I'm doing well, despite this heat from which we get no relief."

"The captain said we're heading into storms tonight and should sail into cooler weather."

"I can hardly wait. Boston was miserable but this boat...well, there's no where to get away from it. Is your wife with you on this trip?"

"She's down in the cabin. She's having the same trouble you are with the heat."

"Does she enjoy all the travel? Or would she rather stay behind and keep up with her social circle in Boston?" Warren wondered what women preferred. He'd never given it much thought. Aunt Louellen hadn't traveled with Uncle Theodore. His mother hadn't traveled with his father. Yet he often met men traveling with their wives. His thoughts strayed to Nellie. He wondered again if she would enjoy traveling with him when he went on business trips. He jerked his thoughts back to his friend.

"My Maria comes as often as she can. She could hardly wait to get out of Boston this time."

"I can imagine. I sent my aunt to the country for her health. I hope she got some relief."

"I heard your aunt has a new companion caring for her in your absence. How is that working out? Your aunt can be…" the man hesitated and then stopped without finishing, as if he'd not meant to say those words aloud.

"Difficult?" Warren finished for him.

The man shrugged but wouldn't meet Warren's eyes.

"Yes, my aunt has a companion now, a young woman from a good family. It's the only way I'd be able to make these trips. My aunt's health isn't what it used to be. The two women get along remarkably well."

"I'm glad to hear it. I remember your uncle, but haven't seen your aunt in years. My wife said she was at a luncheon a couple months ago. I'm ashamed to admit, until she told me about the luncheon, I thought your aunt had passed."

"She had stopped leaving the house. This new companion insists she gets out now and then. She's as stubborn as my aunt and doesn't take 'no' for an answer. It's been good for Aunt Louellen to move in society again. This heat almost killed her. I'm actually quite concerned about her. I've been worried sick about her the last couple days." Warren's mind again drifted to the fact he was missing Nellie with everything in him.

Warren stood. He tucked the handkerchief back into his pocket. "I need to prepare for dinner. I hope to see you then."

"I'm not sure, actually. We took our meal in our room the last two nights. My wife isn't feeling well enough to be up. She may choose to continue resting in our cabin. If she's better, we'll see you tonight. But I'm sure the advent of cooler weather will improve her spirits."

"I hope so." Warren moved away and took the stairs down to his cabin. The tiny room made him feel claustrophobic. He couldn't imagine staying in there all day, every day. Even when he'd been seasick in the past, he'd always gone up on deck to get out of the tight space.

He closed himself in and made a futile attempt to wash off the perspiration. The breeze through the porthole wasn't enough to stir the air. At least inside the room he had relief from the sun's heat.

He sat at the tiny desk situated in the opposite corner of the room from the bed. The distance between was less than a step for him. He pulled out a sheet of paper to write a letter to Nellie and Aunt Louellen.

"My dear Aunt Louellen and Nellie," he began. Then he stopped and crossed off 'my'. He'd have to begin again. He crumpled the paper and tossed it in the trash. He pulled out a clean sheet of paper.

Dear Aunt Louellen and Eleanor,

I trust all is well with you. You've been constantly in my thoughts. I'm hoping the absence of a telegram means Aunt Louellen is feeling better now that you've reached a cooler climate. I hope you are settling into your summer home and you'll enjoy your stay.

I've been on the liner for two days. Two miserable days. The heat has not abated one iota. It feels like a sauna with the sun blinding us from above and the ocean blinding us from below. I heard a rumor we'll reach cooler weather tonight. I'm practically counting the minutes. It feels like we are moving so slowly. Sometimes I look into the gray of the ocean and wonder how difficult it would be to keep up with the ship if I decided to swim along behind. Or maybe I'll swim back to Boston, catch a train, and join you all in Maine. I'm longing to be there with you. At this point, it's hard to know if I'm longing for it only because I wish for some relief from the heat, or if I'm homesick for the two of you. It's safe to say I want to see you more than anything.

A cool breeze fluttered the curtain and blew a loose sheet of paper off the desk onto the floor. The light pouring in the porthole abated enough that Warren looked up from the letter he was writing. Thick dark clouds had obscured the sky in the west. The breeze coming in the window cooled the air in the room. Warren sucked in a relieved breath and turned back to his letter.

It looks like a storm in blowing in from the west, bringing welcome relief. I can only hope it lasts until we reach London. I look forward to finding a letter from you there. Please take care. You are in my thoughts every moment of every day.

Warren washed one more time before dressing for dinner. By the time he left his cabin, the stiff wind carried the smell of rain and the temperature had cooled enough that Warren was thankful for his dinner jacket.

Chapter Twenty-two

Nellie didn't get a chance to sit down and write Warren until late that evening. She used the desk in the drawing room since her mother was already in bed upstairs in her room. She sat for a long time thinking about what she'd tell him. She'd been contemplating it all day, but now the words simply wouldn't come.

Dear Mr. Burke,

I'm so happy to tell you that Aunt Louellen is much improved since we traveled up here yesterday. She slept most of the trip on the train (as did Sophia; running the dog in the garden worked like a charm to tire her out and help her sleep). Yesterday, she ate a good meal for the first time in days. This morning, she slept until almost noon.

I had the fortune of meeting Dr. Grey, our local physician, when we got off the train last night. He's met your aunt and she liked him. He said he'd drop by to check on her as often as we like, at least a couple times a week.

We found a lady in town who will cook for us. Her daughter will clean house and do the wash a couple days a week. This is a relief of mind to me. You know my track record with laundry.

We had a lovely rain last night. Everything here smells so fresh and new. I'm eager to take your aunt to the ocean in the next day or two. I think she'll love it.

I hope you are well, Mr. Burke. I keep seeing things here that I wish I could show you. There are so many places I think you would enjoy. Maybe you'll get time to come visit up here someday. It's lovely. I'd forgotten how lovely it is. I've been away too long.

Nellie finished the letter, folded it and slid it in an envelope. It felt light. She decided she'd write him again the next day and include both in the same envelope. He'd said he wouldn't get any of them until he got to London. What difference would it make if he got more than one at a time?

Aunt Louellen didn't sleep as long the next morning, but she still didn't rise until the sun was high in the sky. Then, she and Nellie took Sophia for a walk around town. Nellie showed her the grocers, the church, and the post office. They finished on the street where Nellie's Gran had lived. Nellie showed Aunt Louellen Gran's quaint little house. It had been repainted and the porch had been repaired, but little else had changed. Nellie felt a tear slide down her cheek as she regarded the house.

"She must have been dear to you," said Aunt Louellen, showing more sympathy than normal.

"Not as dear as she should have been. She was a voice of wisdom for me and I ignored her when it mattered most. Now it's too late to get her advice or express my regrets. I wish I could talk things over with her again. It's easy to get lost in regret and wishful thinking when I dwell on it."

"You and I are doers, not discussers," said Aunt Louellen with a sniff. "We like to act. Or we stubbornly refuse to act. Either way, we don't need to know what other people think because we've already made up our mind. It's good to be decisive, you know."

"We can be, and have been, wrong, Auntie. Like you about sticking it out through the hot weather in Boston. Or me about marrying Philip or Edward. Both were foolhardy ideas and we were silly to be stubborn about them."

Aunt Louellen laughed her dusty laugh and let Nellie lead her back toward Main Street. "You're right, you know. If it had been up to me, I'd probably already be dead from the heat. But I feel revitalized and refreshed here. What heavenly smell is coming from that building?" She stopped in front of the bakery.

Nellie and Aunt Louellen made their way home that afternoon with a cake for dessert and sweet rolls for breakfast.

"I can see I'm going to have to increase the distance I walk if we're going to include the bakery in our route."

Nellie laughed merrily at this. "I've been thinking the same thing, Auntie."

Elaine left the next day. She rode to Walton with Dr. Grey when he went to do his rounds in the hospital there. She hugged Nellie before she left. "Send word and I can be here to help you within hours. Please don't hesitate to send for me if you need me."

"We'll be fine, Mama. But I will be in touch. I can't promise to write every day, but I'll try to do better than I did before."

"Which was never," said her mother with a wink. "Write Meg, too. She'd love to hear from you."

"In all my spare time."

"As much as Mrs. McGowen is sleeping, you might have more time than you think."

Elaine climbed into Dr. Grey's car. He pulled away from the house. Nellie waved until she couldn't see them anymore. Sophia scampered around her legs, so Nellie decided to take her on a romp through the woods.

The woods were lovely this early in the morning. Dew clung to the flowers and dripped off the leaves. The dog ran through the trees as fast as she could then ran back to Nellie.

Nellie stumbled into a clearing and found a patch of Mayflowers under the shade of a tree. She'd never seen them so late in the season. She picked a bouquet to take back to the house. She called Sophia and the two of them started back to town.

When she reached home, Nellie put the flowers in a small vase. She removed the biggest, prettiest mayflower out of the bouquet. She pressed this flower between the pages of the biggest dictionary she could find on their bookshelves. Once it was dry, she'd include it in a letter to Mr. Burke.

A light tap sounded on the back door. Nellie hurried through the house to answer it. Emily stood outside.

"Good morning, Miss Greene," she said.

"Please. Don't call me that," Nellie said with her nose wrinkled up. "Call me Nellie."

"I don't know what Mama would say about it," said the girl. "She would want me to call you Miss Greene. Maybe when I'm here I'll call you Nellie. I'll have to remember to call you Miss Greene at home."

"Now that I think about it, you'd better call me Eleanor. Aunt Louellen insists on it. She says my nickname is vulgar. You do whatever you want. I'll try to remember to answer to it."

Emily surveyed the room to see what needed to be done. Nellie could see the uncertainty on the girl's face. She sprang to the rescue.

"We need you to help with the cleaning and wash. I'll lend a hand with whatever needs to be done but I'll need to spend time with Aunt Louellen when she's awake."

"So, start on the dishes and floors?" asked Emily.

Nellie blushed. Her mother had been doing the dishes the last few days and didn't seem to mind. Nellie hadn't done them yet today. It had been her least favorite job growing up. "Yes. Dishes and floors. But I can work on the floors until Aunt Louellen gets up."

Emily was a few years younger than Nellie, but Nellie could tell she was used to giving directions to her younger sisters. In a matter of minutes she was chattering away to Nellie, interspersing directions in her comments. Nellie swept the kitchen floor. Emily mopped it when she was finished. She put the clothes in the washing machine and the two girls took turns cranking it. Then Nellie helped her put the clothes through the wringer.

Aunt Louellen wandered into the kitchen in search of breakfast just as Emily was ready to carry the clothes out to the line and hang them. Nellie left the girl to her work.

"I can't believe how much I'm sleeping here," said Aunt Louellen. "It's so quiet. The air is so fresh. The bed is the most comfortable bed I've slept in in years. I feel like a lazy old woman right now." As if to emphasize her point, she hid a yawn behind her hand.

Chloe hurried into the kitchen and the two women went in search of food for breakfast. Nellie slipped into the drawing room to write another note to Mr. Burke. She wanted to post it when she took Aunt Louellen for a walk.

Dear Mr. Burke,

My mother has left for Boston. We three ladies are left here to fend for ourselves. Mrs. Stuart, the lady I told you about in my last letter, has been cooking for us. Her daughter came to clean today. You'll be happy to know she's teaching me how to do laundry properly without rubbing holes in the clothes.

Aunt Louellen continues to improve. We walked around Hollis yesterday and I showed her the sights. I think it wore her out because she slept late again this morning.

They've opened the most wonderful bakery in Hollis. Aunt Louellen and I walked past yesterday when the sweet rolls were coming out of the oven. Guess what we had for breakfast this morning? Aunt Louellen said she'd take another long walk today to keep fit since we aren't eating our usual breakfast of porridge. I could do without porridge for a while, especially when I can get sweet rolls and muffins still warm from the oven.

It's already warmer today than it was yesterday, which means we'll need to take a trip to the beach. We'll be thinking of you as we stare across the huge expanse of water, wondering where you are and how you are doing.

Chapter Twenty-three

Dear Aunt Louellen and Nellie,

A passing boat brought the post, including your letters from when you first arrived in Hollis. I'm happy to hear your health is improved, Aunt. It's a relief of mind to me.

We've finally had some relief in the weather. Frightful storms passed over us the other night. They came around dinner time. The ship pitched and rolled, and rain lashed the decks. Many people who'd already come to dinner had to leave because they were ill. I'll admit I didn't handle it well myself. I hadn't eaten anything before it got bad. I was able to get back to my cabin, but I spent most of the night both wishing for and fearing death. A body can only tolerate so much pitching and rocking. I eventually went to sleep and slept past breakfast in the morning. I didn't mind. My stomach and I still weren't in complete agreement. I was able to dress and go out on the deck while others were still confined to their cabins. It rained for the rest of the day, a welcome relief from the heat of the past weeks.

Since then, the weather has been pleasant, not as oppressive as it was. I'm on board with a business acquaintance and we're passing a pleasant time together. We've been playing a lot of deck tennis. He's better at it than I am, though I'm improving. I'm reading the Agatha Christie book you insisted I bring, Aunt. You're correct, once you start it's difficult to stop. I should have brought more reading material. They brought the latest newspapers with the post. I'll make sure to get my turn with one of them in the next few days.

∞

Dear Mr. Burke,

We passed a rainy day yesterday. It was raining when we woke and still raining when we went to bed. We were actually cold! Though I thought about lighting a fire in the drawing room, we decided to wear sweaters and add blankets to the beds. Sophia was miserable. She's grown accustomed to romping in the forest whenever she wants. She would whine to go out and we'd let her. Moments later, she'd whine to come back inside because she was wet and cold. We finally confined her to the drawing room except for her necessaries.

Mrs. Stuart is a wonderful cook. Her food isn't as fancy as Cook's but it's the hearty stuff Aunt Louellen has needed to get over her heat illness. Auntie is getting stronger every day. We still haven't been to the ocean. The rain delayed our plans.

We've taken to reading in the drawing room every evening like we did in Boston. There is a small library on Main Street. Auntie has decided she'll choose something from the library when we've exhausted the few remaining books at my parent's house.

I hope the simple events of our daily life aren't boring to you. You were the one who asked me to write regularly. I promise to try to make it as interesting and enjoyable as possible — within the bounds of what actually happens, of course.

∞

Dear Aunt Louellen and Nellie,

Please don't think anything you do there is boring to me. I want to hear about it. It's not as though my life is particularly exciting or eventful. The days on board the liner blur together with repetitive activity and long hours with nothing to do.

I know you won't get these letters in any sort of order. I'm rushing to get this posted because we're sending mail back with another boat heading to America.

The crew put on a talent show last night. They invited passengers to participate. We have some talented passengers. I, however, am not among them. I sat and watched as people sang, gave speeches or orations, quoted poems. Two people put on a small play. The captain told us they've asked them to organize another play before the end of the voyage.

Saturday night they're having a dance on the deck. They've got a small band on board who'll play popular music. I'm hoping to organize a friendly card game the same evening for those of us whose preference for dancing is dependent on having the right partner.

∞

Dear Mr. Burke,

I'd forgotten how wonderful the ocean is. We've been every day this week. The weather turned hot, but no where as miserable as it was in Boston. The nights have remained cool.

We ride to the beach with Mr. Miller when he fetches produce from local farms. Chloe and I ride in the back of the truck and Aunt Louellen rides in the cab with Mr. Miller. She almost refused to go the first time she saw the conveyance. I insisted she try it once and told her she never had to do it again if she hated it. She's never complained again. He takes a couple hours to make his rounds. He drops us off on his way and picks us up on the way back. Sometimes Emily Stuart comes with us.

Aunt Louellen usually sits on a blanket under an umbrella so she doesn't get too much sun. Yesterday we convinced her to step into the ocean with us. She stayed at the edge for a long time, where the water could roll over her feet. Chloe and Emily and I love to run in and out in our swimming dresses. Aunt Louellen says it isn't proper for young women to act that way. We go in anyway since there's never anyone out with us.

Auntie also insists we take care with our complexions. It isn't ladylike to get a tan, you know. It might be too late for me. I fear I have a tan already. Chloe had a sunburn and peeled. Emily is still young. She already had a tan and doesn't seem concerned about it.

Sometimes I like to sit on the beach and watch the waves roll in. I wonder if any of the water is some you've seen from your liner. I wonder what you're doing and if you're tired of being on the boat. You only have a day or two left of your trip. I'm sure you're eager to be on dry land again.

∞

Dear Aunt Louellen and Nellie,

We should dock in England tomorrow if all goes well and the weather holds. I think the captain will dock regardless of the weather. At least I hope he will. The long days on board the boat are wearing on everyone. I'll take the train to London. I'll be so thankful to sleep somewhere that isn't rocking.

I heard the dance was nice. A swell came up and I was confined to my room with seasickness. So much for a friendly card game, eh? We've played cards a few other times, but the weather has turned gray and damp. We've had fog several mornings until the sun rose and burned it off.

I finished my book days ago. The papers contain old news.

Sadly, that's all I have to tell you. Once I get to London, and then the continent, my activities will increase. Until then, the ocean entertains me with wave after endless wave.

∞

Dear Mr. Burke,

I'm enclosing a mayflower I found late in the season here. I pressed it between two dictionary pages until it dried. I know it needed to stay there longer, but I'm eager to send it. They're such delicate, pretty flowers, and they smell heavenly when they're in season. Hopefully some of the scent lingers on the paper and envelope until you get it so you can enjoy it as well.

We found strawberries in the woods the other day. Aunt Louellen and I have been walking to the patch and picking the ripe ones every day. We found a blackberry patch but they aren't ripe yet and Aunt Louellen isn't eager to fight the thorns. I'm trying to talk Chloe into going with me to pick them, but she's too much a city girl. Emily says her sisters will help pick. Now to be patient until they're ready. I check them every day.

The new pastor of the church here in Hollis is a nice man. Aunt Louellen invited him and his wife for tea the other afternoon. His name is Philby. Walter Philby. He preaches lovely sermons on Sundays. Aunt Louellen debated several points of doctrine with him. She told me later she was testing him to see if he was sound. He must have passed because she's already planning the next time they come for tea.

We're reading Charles Dickens every evening. My father had several he'd left here. Aunt Louellen says he's too depressing for such a lovely place in the world. But she wants to find out what happens and won't let me quit reading.

∞

Dear Aunt Louellen and Nellie,

I've arrived in London and what a relief it is to be off that boat. Hopefully the post reaches you more reliably. I received two letters from you upon my arrival. I envy you your beach excursions. Aunt can tell you, Nellie, we loved going to the shore in the summer. Those are my favorite memories. Your letter makes me want to get on the next boat home and join you. But my business will not take care of itself so I must remain here.

A colleague of mine invited me to his daughter's recital at the conservatory. Aunt Louellen, you would have loved it. They picked pieces from all your favorites. His daughter is a violinist who is auditioning for the London Philharmonic. Maybe one day they'll visit Boston and we can get tickets to hear them.

I attended a lecture the other night as well. Two professors were debating the metaphysical. I must still be adjusting to the new time because I fell asleep almost as soon as they began. The person next to me woke me when I began snoring so I snuck out and returned to my rooms to get a proper night's sleep.

If all continues to go as it has been, I'll be leaving London a full week sooner than I planned. I'll leave a forwarding address, but if you get this in time, you should start sending letters to the second address on the list I gave you, Nellie.

∞

Dear Mr. Burke,

Paris! I've always wanted to see Paris. I've seen photos of the city but I'd imagine it's far better in real life than in a photo. I hope you are enjoying yourself and aren't solely focused on business. It's hard to believe you're there, walking through those places I've only imagined — the Eiffel Tower, the Louvre, the Opera, pastry shops, and couturier. I've dreamed of having a real couture dress from a Paris shop. Right now, in this quiet village, a fancy dress seems like an unnecessary extravagance. Maybe it is. A girl can dream, can't she?

We've been enjoying ourselves. We've been outside so much that even Aunt Louellen is getting a tan despite her best efforts to prevent it. Sophia will never want to return to her life indoors. She's no longer a fat dog. She's lean and fast. She brought us a mouse the other morning while we were eating our porridge — yes, we've begun eating porridge for breakfast most mornings. Our waistlines are thanking us. We all screamed when we saw the mouse, except Emily, who took it in stride and disposed of it. She had a bit of trouble getting the disgusting creature away from the dog. I guess the mouse had been plaguing her in the pantry, leaving messes and generally being a nuisance. Emily was happy to see it gone. I didn't know dogs could be mousers.

Aunt Louellen says to bring back some of the Chanel No. 5 perfume we're reading about in all the magazines. Reynolds has been sending the subscriptions up here for us. She is curious about the scent. The magazines make it sound like the height of sophistication.

Dear Aunt Louellen and Nellie,

The Chanel No. 5 is tucked away in a trunk awaiting my return. It's a new scent, quite popular, and I had trouble acquiring a bottle of it. It's helpful to know someone who knows someone...well, you understand what I mean.

I am doing more than just business. A colleague took me to the Louvre yesterday. The art was amazing, the building itself even more so. We're going to the opera tonight. Tomorrow, I should wrap up my business here and move on to Florence. I had planned to stay longer in Paris, but everything is moving more efficiently than anticipated. I'm ahead of schedule.

Ever since receiving your last letter, Nellie, I've thought of you every time I've gone anywhere or done anything. I pass hat or shoe stores and think how much you'd enjoy seeing the wares. I taste the pastry and wish I could bring some back for you all there. I'm happy you have a bakery in Hollis, but nothing can compare to these delicacies that melt in your mouth. You would adore the Eiffel Tower. I hope you get to come to Paris one day. I know you'll enjoy it.

∞

Dear Mr. Burke,

I know I promised to write often, but this last week has truly been boring. It rained every single day, all day. It would stop at night, then begin again as soon as the sun rose. By the third day cooped up indoors we were all irritable with one another. Auntie and I fought for the first time in weeks. She wanted to take a day trip to Walton. I knew we'd never make it out of town on the soggy roads. As it was, Dr. Grey settled it for us. He slogged his way over to check on us and said he had gotten stuck a mile outside town. It had taken an hour and three big men to get him unstuck. So that was that. We decided to hunker down and endure it as best we could.

I was so thankful to wake this morning to sunshine pouring down my window instead of rain. It's promising to be hot today, but I'll take it. Maybe I'll walk up to the bakery and get us breakfast instead of that awful porridge. Anything to get out of this tiny house. Besides, hearing about the pastries in Paris has made me crave Mrs. Griffin's treats even more.

The blackberries are finally ripe. Hopefully the rain hasn't spoiled them. We plan to pick as many as we can and make them into preserves, which we will then take back to Boston with us. My stomach is growling when I think about them. Maybe I should go see about breakfast.

∞

Dear Aunt Louellen and Nellie,

As lovely as Europe is, I'm finding myself restless and eager to be away. Florence, while wonderful, was quite a lot warmer than I remembered from my last visit. The coffee, however, was exactly the same — delicious in every respect.

Here in Geneva, the Alps are already covered in snow at the higher elevations. They may be in for a cold winter. I'm staying at a lovely hotel next to a lake. I took a boat out rowing yesterday. The day before, I hiked as far up the mountain as I could, leaving enough time to get back for dinner. I love the mountains far more than any of the cities I've visited. They are restful and steadfast. The air here is so clear and fresh. And cool, which is a blessing after the heat in Florence.

I'll be returning home ahead of schedule. It was a simple matter to rearrange the tickets. If you get this before my arrival, please don't change your schedule and return to Boston sooner. Aunt Louellen needs all the fresh, cool air she can get. You are both in my every thought.

Chapter Twenty-four

Warren had never been so restless in his life, but his was a new sort of restlessness. Before, he'd always been eager to travel, go out, see the world, experience new things.

Now, as he hiked the mountain trail for the third time in two weeks and stared back across the valley below him, he felt what he really wanted was to share all of this with someone.

He pulled his handkerchief out of his pocket and mopped his forehead with it. His fingers slipped into the holes Nellie had rubbed. He missed her with every part of himself. Would she enjoy the strenuous exercise involved in hiking these paths? Her letters spoke of long walks in the Maine woods. He thought she would enjoy the mountain hikes. Would she enjoy rowing on the lake? Would she enjoy touring old castles or seeing paintings by famous artists? What about the canals in Florence? He knew she hoped to see all of it one day and he wanted to be the one to show her.

He made his way down the mountain and dressed for dinner. He'd be leaving first thing in the morning by train. He'd reach London in a couple days and board his return liner at the end of the week. He felt a certain measure of relief that he'd accomplished his goals ahead of schedule and could return to the people who had never been far from his thoughts.

He could hardly wait to get back.

Warren's fingertips passed over the collection of items he'd chosen for Nellie and Aunt Louellen on his travels. Two bottles of perfume, lace gloves, a china teacup and Earl Grey tea, a first edition of a novel by F. Scott Fitzgerald that he'd had signed by the author in Paris for Nellie. He hoped she'd enjoy it as much as the Agatha Christie novel he was bringing back with him. There was a famous chocolatier he planned to visit on the way back. Both Aunt Louellen and Nellie would enjoy the treat.

Nellie had written faithfully, but impersonally, all summer. Her letters had shared what they did every day, but not how she felt. He'd hoped their letters would grow more personal as time passed. He also knew he didn't dare say too much in his in case Aunt Louellen read them instead of Nellie. She must have feared the same thing.

In the meantime, he'd been pouring out his thoughts for her in a journal all summer. He'd gotten the leather-bound book in a bookshop in London the first possible chance he'd had.

That was the same day he'd gotten her the teacup. He'd passed a small tea shop. The cup had been sitting in the window. It had pink roses on a green background. Warren could picture Nellie's eyes when she saw it for the first time, when she lifted it to her full lips to take a sip, her eyes meeting his across the drawing room.

He stopped his train of thoughts. He was in danger of building her up to be a different person than she was in reality. That said, he loved the vivacious enthusiasm that came across in her letters. That was real. Her determination was real. Her ability to influence Aunt Louellen for good was real.

His plan was simple. He'd travel to Boston and check with his manager to make sure all was in order to receive the shipments. Then he'd join Aunt Louellen and Nellie in Hollis. He'd be able to see the place for himself. He planned to surprise them. The prospect filled him with nervous excitement.

Nellie and Aunt Louellen took their usual morning walk around Hollis. They waved to Rev. Philby who was weeding his garden. Most of the summer vegetables were finished, but there were still a few late tomatoes and green beans clinging to the vines. She could see where he'd planted his fall squash. One green pumpkin was already rather large.

The smell of fresh bread wafted out of the bakery.

"We could stop to get some of those lovely, crusty, yeast rolls to eat with the stew Mrs. Stuart brought over," Aunt Louellen suggested.

"They do smell heavenly, don't they. Mrs. Stuart brought bread to eat with it."

"We'll have it for breakfast tomorrow instead of porridge, along with the blackberry preserves you put up."

Nellie took in the rosy cheeked, bright-eyed face of the elderly lady beside her. Aunt Louellen's walk had grown more confident. She held herself more erect. She hadn't used the cane in weeks, though sometimes she would hold their arm when she walked across the sand at the beach. She was stronger than she had been since Nellie had met her.

Sophia tugged on the lead in Aunt Louellen's hand and she resisted. "Make a decision. Sophia won't wait all day."

Nellie raised an eyebrow. "Sophia, heel," she commanded. The little dog scampered back to Aunt Louellen's side. "You need to give her the commands now and then, Auntie." She hesitated outside the bakery door. "I'll go in and get the rolls and catch up with you."

"Take as long as you need, dear. Sophia and I know where to go." Aunt Louellen continued her confident stride up Main Street and turned the corner toward home.

Nellie ducked into the bakery. Several ladies were in line ahead of her, including Mrs. Miller, the grocer's wife, and Mrs. Philby. The three women chatted about the upcoming fall program. They'd begun teaching the town children songs for it. Mrs. Philby wanted them to do a tableau of the First Thanksgiving, but Mrs. Miller was uncertain.

By the time Nellie had the rolls they needed and a danish for each of them (they were fresh from the oven and smelled so wonderful; she told herself she'd serve them for tea that afternoon, while they were still warm and soft) Aunt Louellen was long gone. Nellie hurried toward home the shortest way, knowing Aunt Louellen had probably already arrived.

A sleek, black car slid past on the cobblestone road. Who could have driven to town in such a nice car? Did Dr. Grey get a new one? He'd been complaining his old rattletrap wasn't long for this world but had made no mention of replacing it. With a flash of embarrassment, Nellie realized she was staring like a country bumpkin and hurried forward. She turned the corner onto her street. The car cruised past again.

Suddenly, it stopped. A man opened the back door and jumped out. Nellie shrank back, trying to decide if she should run home, or back to Main Street.

Then she realized the man was Warren Burke.

With a glad cry, and not a thought for who might be watching, she dropped her basket and threw herself into his open arms.

He was laughing. He lifted her and spun her in a circle, then set her on the ground. "Look at you," he breathed. His eyes covered her face like a caress. A moment later, his fingers stroked her cheek. "It wouldn't be proper to kiss you out here, in public." His voice was so quiet, Nellie feared she hadn't heard him right. Then his thumb traced her lips.

Nellie covered his hand with her own. "I've missed you. We didn't expect to see you until we returned to Boston."

As if coming to his senses, Mr. Burke released Nellie and stepped back. "Is your parent's house close?"

"It's that one, there." Nellie pointed to the house up the street.

Mr. Burke retrieved the basket Nellie had dropped and motioned for the driver to follow. He offered Nellie his arm. When she slipped her hand into the crook of his elbow, he took her fingers and held them with his other hand.

"I decided to come back early. Your letters were so compelling, I wanted to see the place for myself."

"You chose *this*," Nellie waved her hand at their surroundings, "over Europe?"

Mr. Burke chuckled at her evident shock. Then he grew serious and squeezed her fingers. He brought his face ever so much closer to hers. "No, I chose *this* over Europe." He lifted her fingers and kissed them.

Nellie flushed and looked away.

"You thought I'd forget you over the summer, didn't you?"

"It's happened before," Nellie said with a shrug. She couldn't meet his gaze, though she wanted to.

"Miss Greene...Nellie, look at me."

Mr. Burke's soft command brought Nellie's eyes to his. They'd reached the house and were standing outside, the afternoon sun casting long shadows over the front of the house. Nellie searched Mr. Burke's face and saw nothing had changed since those last moments they'd had together in Boston weeks ago.

"You were always in my thoughts. Europe wasn't as interesting as before because I wanted you to see everything I was seeing. I wanted to experience it with you."

"Do you realize what you're saying, Mr. Burke?" Nellie whispered.

"Yes," he breathed back. "But I also realize my aunt still needs you and will for some time to come. We don't have to figure it all out right now. I'm so happy to be with you again. And you need to start calling me

Warren." He kissed her fingers once more. "We'd better get inside, before Aunt gets suspicious."

Nellie finally dragged her eyes away from his and led the way around the back of the house to the kitchen door. They could hear Sophia barking on the other side. She opened the door into the kitchen.

Aunt Louellen had settled in her usual place at the head of the kitchen table. Chloe sat next to her and Emily was filling the tea pot at the stove. The three women stopped and stared as they entered.

"Warren," said Aunt Louellen with a stiff smile. "I see you've arrived safely from your trip. We wondered since we hadn't heard from you in a while."

Mr. Burke…Warren, leaned and gave his aunt his customary peck on the cheek. "You would have heard if something bad had happened, I assure you. I decided to come for a visit. Your letters described a place I decided I needed to see with my own eyes."

Nellie saw Emily was blushing furiously. The kettle clattered against the stove top and she apologized. Nellie took the china tea pot from her before she could drop it and placed it on the table. "We'll need more water for our tea tonight. Refill the pot so it can heat again. I'll put the danishes I bought on a plate. Do we still have some of the berry muffins from yesterday? Because I didn't buy enough danishes."

Emily, still speechless, scrambled for the kettle and filled it. Then she hurried to the pantry for the muffins. "You have enough if I go," she whispered to Nellie.

"You must stay. You always stay. Why would tonight be any different?" Nellie whispered back.

Emily cut a glance at Warren. Her cheeks glowed red. "I can't."

"He won't bite, I promise. Take a deep breath and calm down. Then have tea with us like always." Nellie placed her hand on the girl's shoulder to calm her.

Emily finally met Nellie's eyes and giggled. "He's way more handsome and sophisticated than I imagined."

"You need to get out more," Nellie said with a shake of her head.

They carried the food to the table and sat down for tea.

Warren regaled them with stories of his trip and things he'd seen. Even Aunt Louellen listened with interest.

After supper, Chloe helped Aunt Louellen to bed while Nellie cleared the supper dishes and washed them.

Warren watched from the other side of the table. He'd removed his jacket and tie and rolled his sleeves to his elbows — much less formal than he would have been for dinner in Boston.

"All this domesticity looks good on you," he said. He grinned when Nellie glowered in mock offense and threw a towel at him.

"The least you could do is dry the dishes while you mock me," she said.

Warren laughed but joined her next to the sink without complaint.

"I've even learned how to do laundry," Nellie said. "I could wash your handkerchief without putting a hole in it."

Warren stepped close behind her. "I carried that handkerchief with me everywhere when I was traveling."

"Why? I ruined it. You said you have many others you could use." Nellie felt his breath on her ear and it sent pleasant shivers down her spine.

"Because it felt like I had a piece of you close to me," he whispered.

Nellie wanted nothing more than to lean into Warren's chest and feel him wrap his arms around her again. The old Nellie would have taken advantage of the situation. She would have leaned into Warren and flirted with him. Nellie didn't want to be that person anymore. She didn't want to manipulate him.

She had to be careful. She was in love with Warren Burke. She'd realized it tonight when she recognized him on the street. The realization had been accompanied by the knowledge that, in her previous relationships, she'd only been in love with the idea of marriage. It hadn't mattered to whom, or if they loved her in return. She'd been so desperate to be married she'd thrown herself at the men she'd imagined were interested. This time had to be different. This time, she had to patiently wait for Warren to lead. She couldn't force it, no matter how much she wanted to do so.

Part of her regretted throwing herself at him in the road earlier in the evening. She should have been more restrained, more ladylike, as Aunt Louellen was always reminding her. But she knew she hadn't imagined his joy upon seeing her.

It took everything in her but Nellie stepped away from Warren on the pretense of grabbing a dirty pan from the stove. She scrubbed it harder than necessary, taking out her frustration and longing on the guiltless pan.

Warren stepped to the side and took the pan from her when she'd finished scouring it. He searched Nellie's face for a moment, holding her gaze, refusing to turn away, until Nellie flushed and returned her attention to the dishpan in front of her.

"I wish I could have shared more in my letters. There were things I saw and did I knew you would appreciate. Aunt Louellen wouldn't have understood. She would have said it was inappropriate to write to you in such a manner." Warren set the dry pan on the stove and reached for the first in the stack of plates.

Nellie glanced up at him. "There were things I wish I could have shared in my letters, but didn't for the same reason. I enjoyed your letters very much. I loved hearing about the places you visited. We all watched for their arrival."

"I had hoped your letters would give me a chance to get to know you, Nellie. I want to learn about you, the things you like and dislike, your goals and ambitions."

"I think you're aware of all of those things already," said Nellie.

"You are more than the woman the gossips think you are. You're a smart, strong, thoughtful woman who is willing to put her life on hold to care for an old woman."

Nellie felt her face flush deep red but she fixed her gaze on the dishpan. Warren probably knew as much about her as anyone. "I don't know much about you," she finally managed.

"I wrote this to help you get to know me." Warren hung the towel on the rack beside the sink and grabbed his jacket from the hook beside the back door. He pulled a leather journal from his pocket and handed it to Nellie. "There were so many things in my heart that never made it into my letters. I wrote the things I thought and felt in here. Consider it my letters to you alone from Europe.

"Peters is taking me back to Walton tonight. I got a room there when it became evident I wouldn't be able to find anything here."

Nellie gasped and clapped her hands over her mouth. "Has he been sitting in the car this whole time?"

"He said he brought the paper."

"He needs food!"

She hurried to the pantry and brought thick slices of bread. She spread them with blackberry preserves. Then she found a small tin container her father had used to carry food with him on his rounds. She put the remainder of the soup in it and led Warren out the back door.

The sun hung low on the western horizon. It stained the sky brilliant oranges and pinks that faded to dusky blues. Peters sat on the curb next to the car. He held the paper but was watching the sunset. Nellie hurried to him and handed him the soup.

"Tomorrow night you can come in and eat with us," she said.

The young man grinned up at her. "Thanks, miss. Gimme a minute and I'll leave this here with you."

"You'll have to dry your own dishes," teased Warren. He'd slung his coat over his arm and stuffed his hands in his pockets.

Nellie rolled her eyes at him, but laughed. "I'm more than capable, Mr. Burke. I've had years of practice washing dishes. That was one domestic skill my mother drilled into me, no matter how much I complained about it."

Peters inhaled the food, then rose to leave. He handed the dishes to Nellie with his thanks and got in the car.

"I'll see you tomorrow," said Warren.

"We're going to the beach tomorrow," said Nellie. "We're trying to go as many times as we can before we travel back to Boston."

"Then I'll come prepared for the beach. Peters can drive us."

Nellie shook her head. "We'll get sand all over the inside of the car. No, we can catch a ride with Mr. Miller. I've already made the arrangements. If you're going to come see what we've been doing this summer, you just as well see all of it, including our unorthodox means of transportation."

"As usual, your logic wins the day." Warren grinned at Nellie. He leaned closer, as though he was going to kiss her.

Nellie wanted him to kiss her, more than anything. But not here. Not where everyone could watch. Not where people might talk. She turned her face and his lips brushed her cheek.

Warren caught her chin and forced her gaze to meet his. Whatever he saw there gave him pause. He gave her a smile. "Until tomorrow morning." Then he hopped into the car and it slid away in the dark.

Chapter Twenty-five

Nellie overslept the next morning. She woke to the sound of the others talking and laughing in the kitchen below her.

She'd been up far too late the night before reading the journal from Warren. All she wanted to do was to pull the covers over her head and go back to sleep. Instead, with the covers in place, she found some of the passages in the journal running through her mind. A pleased warmth spread through her. She smiled in the semi-darkness of her blanket den.

He had missed her. Nellie had been afraid he'd forget all about her, but instead, he'd gotten so homesick he'd come home early. She thought about his final entry.

I've traveled for work my entire adult life. My uncle gave the business to my father who gave it to me. I've always loved it — seeing new places, meeting new people, trying new food. My mother wanted me to settle down and get married. She couldn't understand my wanderlust. I hadn't met a woman compelling enough to keep me in one place for long.

But I was doing it wrong. I think I've met a woman, you Eleanor, who will enjoy wandering with me. I appreciate your decisive opinions and the fact that you know your own mind and aren't afraid to state it. Your taste is impeccable. You know how to spot the quality products I've brought back to sell. I enjoy hearing you read to Aunt Louellen with such life and vigor inserted into the stories.

I've never met another woman who made me want to come home like you have. That's the strange thing. Before I met you, no place felt like home. Now, when I think of home, I think of you. I'm longing to see you and see where you grew up, the place that made you who you are. That's why I've wrapped up my business early — so I could travel back and visit Maine while you're still there.

Nellie shoved the covers off and got up. She could hardly wait to see Warren this morning. He'd be there any time to go to the beach with them. She dressed and hurried downstairs for breakfast.

Aunt Louellen looked at her askance as she entered the kitchen. "You slept much later than normal. Are you feeling alright?" She glared at Nellie, as if taking personal offense that Nellie had overslept.

"I stayed up late reading," Nellie explained. She helped herself to some coffee and porridge and settled at the table. She watched Aunt Louellen while she ate. The old woman's movements and words sounded sluggish and her hand shook. But when she stood and walked to her room, everything seemed fine.

They made their picnic lunch and were waiting at the road when Warren arrived. Mr. Miller was not far behind. Mr. Miller helped Aunt Louellen into the cab. She clung to him longer than usual, as though she was struggling to catch her balance. Nellie watched until she was safely seated, then went around to the back of the truck where the girls piled in as usual. Warren watched, amused. He glanced down at his clean trousers and back at the girls in the truck.

"Climb on in," said Nellie. "A little dirt won't kill you."

Warren cocked an eyebrow at her and stepped onto the bumper as the truck lurched forward. Warren grabbed the side rail just in time. The girls shrieked as Warren tumbled into the back of the truck. He came up laughing, the entire front of him covered in dirt.

"Mr. Burke!"

"Are you okay?"

"Don't worry, the dirt will wash out."

All three girls spoke at once. Nellie brushed at his shirt. The dusty mess came off easily. Warren caught her hands to stop her fussing.

"I'm fine. It's a little dirt. Nothing to be worried about. I brought a change of clothes in the car. You can demonstrate your laundry skills when we get back." He held her hands a moment longer until Nellie flushed and pulled away. He scooted over to the side of the truck bed so he could see out the front.

"Laundry skills?" asked Emily.

"Mr. Burke loaned me a handkerchief and I took it upon myself to wash it before I gave it back. I washed two nice sized holes in it. It was quite embarrassing."

Emily laughed merrily. "So when you told me you needed to learn how to do laundry, you meant it."

"Has she improved?" asked Warren.

"Oh, immensely. She hasn't scrubbed holes into anything on my watch."

When they reached the beach, they unloaded everything out of the truck. With a wave to Mr. Miller, they set off across the sand to their favorite spot. Aunt Louellen walked without assistance and Nellie breathed a sigh of relief. She was worrying over nothing. Warren carried the picnic basket and followed Nellie.

The sun beat down while the sand reflected the heat. They were soon sweating. Chloe and Emily changed into their swimming dresses and ran into the water. They filled the air with their shrieks. Nellie walked with Sophia along the water line until a wave washed over her feet. The cold water made her gasp and jump back. She returned to the blanket and Aunt Louellen.

“Aren’t you two going to join them?” Aunt Louellen asked.

“The water is freezing, Auntie. I don’t know how those two are managing it,” Nellie said. She extended her feet so they could dry in the hot sun.

“I’ll be the judge of that,” said Aunt Louellen. She struggled to stand and walked down to the water’s edge.

“It’s beautiful here,” said Warren. “I understand why you spent so much of the summer here.”

“I love it,” said Nellie. She gazed across the expanse of ocean, the endless, mesmerizing waves washing over the beach, the lap and splash of the water, the tangy, salty, fishy smell carried on the breeze. “When you were traveling on the liner, I used to wonder if any of the water we saw washing up here had passed you. Maybe you’d seen it first.” She fiddled with her fingers in her lap then waved her hand dismissively. “It’s silly.”

"It's not silly. I find it gratifying you were thinking of me when you were here. Are you going to swim?"

"I don't know," said Nellie.

"Well I'm planning to try it out. You should come with me."

"It's freezing," Nellie warned again.

"Then I'll have to try not to catch my death. Good thing we've got a nice hot day today."

They walked down the beach to the water. Aunt Louellen was searching for shells. Sophia ran in and out of the water, barking at the gulls. Chloe and Emily were splashing in the surf.

Warren grabbed Nellie's hand and tugged her toward the water. She resisted, tugging hard against Warren's grip when a larger wave splashed up her legs and soaked her to the waist. She gasped and shrieked, then burst out laughing. Warren started running into the waves, pulling Nellie behind him. When another large one broke right in front of them, he stumbled into it. Nellie fell in along with him. She was soaked through.

"Come on!" he called and began swimming out into the ocean, ducking under the waves. Nellie followed. She'd always been a strong swimmer and she had no trouble keeping up.

Once she got used to it, the cool water felt wonderful in the hot sun. When she grew tired, Nellie turned back to the beach to set out lunch. Chloe was back already and was sprawled on a rock attempting to get dry. Emily was combing the beach for shells Aunt Louellen had missed.

"He's always been fond of the ocean," said Aunt Louellen, observing Warren out in the surf. They watched his head bob up and down in the waves. Aunt Louellen absently stroked Sophia, who'd collapsed at her feet and was sound asleep. She grew serious and turned to face Nellie. "He's a great deal older than you, you know."

"Yes, Auntie, I know," said Nellie. She busied herself with their lunch.

"He's never been interested in women, either."

Nellie wasn't sure where Aunt Louellen was going with this conversation but she nodded and continued what she was doing.

"I don't know why anything would change now."

"What if he met a woman he found compelling?" asked Nellie.

"Do you mean yourself? Because you need to dismiss all thought of that from your mind. I will not have you toying with my nephew the way you did with those other men."

Tears sprang to Nellie's eyes. The hurt she felt at Aunt Louellen's unexpected words was overwhelming. "I never toyed with those men. Why would you say such a thing?" she said.

"You wouldn't be angry if there wasn't some truth to my statement," said Aunt Louellen with a sniff.

"I'm not angry. I'm hurt. There is no truth to your statement and you know it." Nellie was struggling to keep her voice down. Her hands shook and she clenched them in her lap to make them stop. "You've defended me to other people."

"That's before I saw you trying to wheedle your way in with my nephew. Don't think I'm not aware he's the most eligible man in Boston. Wouldn't it look good for you to attach yourself to him? He's a far better catch than those other men ever were." The old woman glared and jabbed her finger at Nellie.

"I don't have to stay here and listen to this," Nellie said. Hot tears threatened and she didn't want to get caught crying.

"Where are you going? Mr. Miller won't be here for another hour. Sit and eat with us. You can tell my nephew you don't appreciate his attention and be done with the whole affair. If you don't, I will. It's as simple as that." Aunt Louellen finished with a haughty sniff and turned her gaze to the ocean, dismissing Nellie.

Nellie sprang to her feet. She grabbed her shoes and hat where she'd dropped them next to the picnic blanket. "I don't have to stay and do anything. We aren't far from Hollis. I'll walk back." She whirled around and stormed up the beach. When the path became pebbly with grasses that cut her bare feet, she sat and put on her stockings and shoes. Then she walked as fast as she could toward the village. Hot tears streamed down her face. The pain was so intense, her chest hurt and her stomach clenched. She cut through a forest path she remembered from her childhood, hoping to avoid anyone seeing her if they drove by on the road.

Chapter Twenty-six

Warren heard raised voices and looked back at the beach. Nellie stood next to the picnic blanket. He watched as she turned on her heel and nearly ran up the beach. He swam back as fast as he could and hurried to his aunt who stroked the dog as if nothing had happened.

"Where is Nellie going?" he asked.

"She's decided she can't stand your company any more today."

"Aunt Louellen, I know that isn't true. Tell me what happened."

"I warned her to stay away from you. For your own good, of course. That girl has a reputation with men."

"Louellen McGowen, how dare you? How dare you meddle in my life and hers in this manner? How dare you mistreat a woman who has done nothing but care for you these last few months? How could you be so unkind?"

"It's for your own good!" Aunt Louellen repeated. "I've seen the way you two look at each other. You think I'm blind and senile but I'm not. I will not have you throw your life and fortune away on that hussy."

Warren jerked back as if he'd been struck. "Take that back."

"I won't. You know it's true."

"And you know it isn't. Yet you said it anyway. You're no different or better than those women back home you claim to despise so much. Take it back."

The old lady's eyes narrowed. "I won't take it back. And you won't be seeing her anymore. I'll disown you. Write you out of my will."

Warren stood. He towered over his aunt and leaned in. "I don't care. I will do what I want. You've threatened this before. You forget, I don't need your money. I thought you'd changed over the last few months. I thought Nellie had been good for you, helped you see life from a different perspective. I was wrong. You're a mean, hateful, awful woman. If you won't apologize to her, I'll be taking her back to Boston with me and I'll make arrangements for Chloe to bring you back. You don't get to treat her like this, or anyone for that matter."

"So you've made your choice."

"Yes, I have. I wish you'd make a better one. Now I need to go find Nellie." Warren ran back toward the road. He had no idea where he was going or how he'd even find her, but he had to try.

He reached the road and turned toward town. She had a long head start on him. Then he noticed the path through the woods. Could it be a shortcut? He had to risk it. He hoped he wasn't getting himself horribly lost.

He plunged through the woods, calling her name. Several minutes later, he could see the light color of her dress through the trees. He called louder. She stopped, hesitated for a moment, then plunged on. Warren followed.

"Nellie! Please! Stop running! We have to talk!" He caught up to her, ran in front of her and stopped. She was crying hard and her face was blotchy and red. She tried to dart around him but he caught her by the waist and pulled her against him. "Don't run away from me, please."

"Your aunt..." she sobbed out against him.

He stroked her hair and tightened his arms. "She told me what she said. I don't know why. Before you came along she did this to anyone and everyone who worked for her. She'd find something to pick at them about and she'd needle them until they either quit or gave her a reason to fire them. You were the first one she didn't treat that way. I don't know why she's turned on you now."

"What she said was true," Nellie gasped against him.

"It's not true. She said it to hurt you. I think she feels like everyone has abandoned her. Years ago, she turned into the kind of person who people wanted to abandon. It's turned into a self-perpetuating cycle."

Warren drew Nellie away from him and took her face in his hands. His eyes bore into hers begging her to see the truth, to believe it. "What she said isn't true."

He wiped a tear away with his thumb. Another followed it. He kissed it away, then another, and another. Then his lips met hers. Nellie melted into him and kissed him back. Her arms tightened around him. Her breath caught when she broke the kiss, but instead of pulling away, she rested her head against his chest. Warren stroked her wet hair and listened to her breathing calm.

After a few minutes, Warren leaned back and stared down at the woman he loved. He cupped her face in his hands, forcing her eyes to meet his. "You don't have to go back to the beach."

Nellie heaved a sigh. "It's not the first time we've fought and it probably won't be the last." She stepped away from him and turned to figure out where they were. "We're still closer to the beach than town. We should probably go back and be ready to help when Mr. Miller gets there."

Warren caught her hand and held it as they walked back the way they'd come.

"My cousin, Meg, and I used to play in these woods when we were children. Her parents would come visit my Gran and we'd run out here and get lost. Or try to get lost. It's almost impossible to do that in these woods."

"Where did your Gran live?"

"I need to show you her house. It's not far. Nothing in Hollis is far from anything else." Nellie gave a weak laugh. Warren could still see pain behind her eyes, but she was trying. He squeezed her hand. "I showed Aunt Louellen Gran's house. Now she likes to walk past there every day."

"What about your cousin?"

"Meg? She got married a couple years ago. I was off feeling sorry for myself and didn't attend. I've regretted that decision ever since. She and her husband live in Indiana. They have a baby. Mama said they'd be coming to visit after the harvest. Her husband farms with his father."

They'd reached the road. The beach wasn't far away. Nellie held back. Warren squeezed her hand again. "You are not the person she's accusing you of being."

"I know that, and you know that, but for some reason, today she doesn't know that."

"She's afraid. She's old and lonely, and she's afraid we'll leave her like everyone else has."

"What she said still hurts."

"I know. Believe me, I told her exactly what I thought about what she said."

"You stood up for me?" Nellie whispered.

"Of course," Warren whispered back. "Why wouldn't I?"

Nellie beamed at him while a lone tear slid down her cheek. She swiped it away, squared her shoulders, and headed down the beach path with Warren following.

They met the other three ladies on the path. Aunt Louellen leaned heavily on Chloe, while Emily tried to manage the blankets and basket. Sophia scampered around their feet, but kept running back to her mistress as if she could tell something wasn't right.

Warren and Nellie hurried forward. Warren lightened Emily's load and Nellie tried to help Chloe. Aunt Louellen didn't fight her. Concern gripped Warren. The old woman's face was gray, her eyes confused.

"I'm glad you came back," she said. "I have the most frightful headache."

"You've probably been out in the sun too long," said Nellie. "It's hot today. I should have taken you back sooner. Warren offered to bring his car. We should have taken him up on the offer."

"Why did you come back for me?" The old woman could barely talk. Her words were slurred. "I was cruel to you back there. Cruel. It was unacceptable." She staggered despite the two women holding her up and sagged onto the ground.

Warren hurried to his aunt. He dropped the things he was carrying and caught her before she fell. In one smooth motion, he swept her into his arms.

"How far is it back to town if you cut through the woods?" he asked Nellie.

"Not far. A mile or so. But you can't carry her all the way. Mr. Miller will be here any minute."

"I know the path," said Emily. "I'll run back and get help."

"Good," said Nellie. "That would be good. See if Dr. Grey is home and have him meet us at the house."

The girl dashed through the trees. Warren and the other two women watched her go, helpless to do anything but wait.

Time dragged on and on as they waited. Aunt Louellen groaned and put her hand to her head. Warren set her on the ground and propped her up while Nellie found something for her to drink in the basket. She drank greedily, then sagged against Warren.

The water seemed to revive her. She squinted up at Nellie, who sponged her face with a damp handkerchief.

"I'm not too hot. My head hurts," Aunt Louellen managed. "It was hurting before we left this morning, but I didn't want to miss our beach excursion. I should have stayed home and rested."

"I'm so sorry, Auntie," said Nellie.

Aunt Louellen caught her hand. "I can't take back what I said. I'll regret it until the day I die. I love you like you're my own grand-daughter. Why, oh! Why am I so cruel to the people I love most and who love me no matter what?" She turned her face to Warren's shoulder and sobbed.

"Now, see here, you have to stop crying," Nellie murmured and stroked Aunt Louellen's hair away from her face. She lifted the water jar to Aunt Louellen's mouth to offer her a drink. The old woman calmed enough to take another sip. "Crying will only make your head hurt worse. Dr. Grey will check you in a few minutes. Everything will be fine."

Warren grew restless with concern. "I could have had her back by now."

"No, it wouldn't be safe to try to carry her through the woods. There are too many roots and rocks in the path." Nellie squeezed his shoulder to reassure him.

The rattle of Mr. Miller's truck reached their ears before they saw him round the bend in the road. Chloe waved him over. The man parked next to them and sprang out of the vehicle.

"What happened?" he cried. "Is she hurt?"

"I think she's sick. It came on suddenly. We need to get her back as soon as we can. Emily ran ahead to fetch Dr. Grey," Nellie said.

Warren lifted his aunt and carried her around to the passenger side of the cab. Chloe was the smallest of the three remaining adults so they decided she would sit next to Aunt Louellen to keep her steady.

The back of the truck was laden with late summer vegetables, the last of the corn and tomatoes, the first of the fall squash. Warren surveyed the load. "Where do we sit?"

Nellie clambered into the back without waiting for help. She plunked onto a crate with a lid nailed on top. "Sit where ever you can find a space and hang on. He usually drives slower on the way back. He doesn't want to break the eggs. But I'm not sure what he'll do today."

Warren handed their belongings up to Nellie, then climbed up beside her. The truck lurched forward. Warren grabbed the edge and wrapped an arm around Nellie's waist. "I don't want to fall out," he said.

Nellie gave a weak laugh but didn't complain.

Mr. Miller took the road faster than normal. Dr. Grey was waiting when they reached the house. He watched Warren lift his aunt from the cab, carry her into the house, and place her on her bed. Sophia followed them into the room. She curled up in a corner and refused to leave.

Warren stood back while Dr. Grey stepped forward. Dr. Grey met his intense, worried stare. "Go tell the ladies I'd appreciate some tea once I've examined Mrs. McGowen. Don't worry, Mr. Burke. I'll take good care of your aunt."

Warren joined the ladies in the kitchen and they waited.

Chapter Twenty-seven

"Your aunt is in good health, aside from what appears to be a severe headache," Dr. Grey told them over a cup of tea. "I've given her some medicine to help with the pain. Here are enough doses of it to get you through the night if she needs it again. She's asking for someone to come help her into her nightdress."

Nellie and Chloe stood at the same time and hurried to Aunt Louellen's side. Nellie took warm water and a towel with her so they could give her a sponge bath before putting her to bed. The two women worked well together after months of practice and soon had Aunt Louellen settled. Nellie gave her another drink before tucking the covers around her throat.

"Sleep," she commanded. "Hopefully you'll feel better when you wake."

Aunt Louellen was unable to resist. The effects of the medicine and headache combined to make her eyelids heavy. Within moments, she was fast asleep.

Nellie returned to the kitchen in time to hear Dr. Grey finish his report.

"We'll treat it a day at a time and keep a close watch on her. If she doesn't improve, we'll need to find a way to get her to the hospital in Walton. But right now, I don't think that's necessary."

Dr. Grey finished his tea and took his leave. Nellie saw him to the door. "You send for me if there is any change for the worse at all. Anything. Day or night. You hear me?"

"I promise," said Nellie.

The kind doctor patted her arm and hurried down the steps.

Nellie returned to the kitchen where everyone sat in stunned silence. "This wasn't how I thought the last week of our stay would go," she said.

The others murmured agreement, then fell silent.

"We need to get cleaned up. Some of us should rest so we can sit with her tonight if she's still sick. I can set up the camp bed in her room if I need to." Nellie had no idea how to proceed. She'd never done well taking care of sick people. Dr. Grey had said to watch Aunt Louellen, so watch her they would.

Warren stood. "I'll sit with her while you all do what you need to do. I won't be able to stay here tonight so I'll take the first shift."

"Thank you," said Nellie. "Don't you want to wash up? She's sleeping right now."

"I'll be fine. Don't worry about me," said Warren with a shrug. "Peters isn't supposed to be back with the car until this evening. I'll sit with her until then."

Aunt Louellen woke once before evening. Nellie encouraged her to drink some broth Emily had made that afternoon. She drank eagerly, but seemed confused about where she was when she finished. She didn't recognize Nellie at first and got upset with Warren when he reminded her. They gave her another dose of the medicine Dr. Grey had left and let her sleep.

Nellie read to her as usual that evening. Warren listened from his seat across the room.

"I love hearing you read," he said when she'd finished. He stood, came to stand behind her, and placed his hands on her shoulders. Nellie leaned her cheek on his arm.

"It's been a long, difficult day," she said. "I wanted something to feel normal."

"I need to leave. I hope when she wakes up, everything is back to the way it was before." Warren leaned and kissed Nellie's cheek. "Good night, my love."

"You've never said that before," Nellie whispered.

"Haven't I? I've thought it often enough. I love you, Eleanor Greene."

"I love you, too, Warren Burke." Nellie was almost afraid to say the words aloud for fear she'd ruin everything. She stood and wrapped her arms around Warren's neck. He didn't kiss her. He didn't need to. They leaned against each other, drawing strength from one another after the difficult day.

"I'll see you in the morning," Warren whispered. He pulled away and let his hand slide down her arm until he held her hand. He squeezed it one last time, then left the room, shutting the door behind him with a soft 'click'.

Nellie sat with Aunt Louellen until Chloe came in to relieve her. She slipped upstairs to her own room and dressed for bed. But, despite the fact she was exhausted from the long emotional day, she couldn't fall asleep. She found herself jumping at every sound, every creak of the boards, every whisper of wind around the house.

Nellie finally gave up and lit the lamp beside her bed. She opened the journal Warren had given her and reread her favorite entries. She grew drowsy, turned off the lamp, and finally fell into a restless sleep.

Chapter Twenty-eight

Scratches at her door jerked Nellie out of the strange dream she was having. She heard a whine, and then more scratches. Was that Sophia? What could be happening? The sky outside her window was stained gray and pink. She grabbed her dressing gown and opened the door. The little dog whined again and scampered down the stairs. She came back for Nellie, then ran down the stairs again. Nellie followed as fast as she could. She peered inside Aunt Louellen's room.

A horrifying sight met her eyes. Aunt Louellen lay sprawled on the floor. Chloe sat next to her head where blood streamed down Aunt Louellen's face.

"She fell out of bed before I could stop her. She was muttering about something and tried to get up. I wanted to help her back into bed but couldn't lift her. Nellie, she can't walk. Her leg is completely useless. Look at her face." Sobs wracked Chloe's body and she had to stop talking.

Nellie dropped to the floor next to Aunt Louellen. The old woman's face beneath the blood was frozen in a half frown. Her lip drooped and a stream of drool slid down her face and into the lace of her nightgown.

Nellie scrambled back to her feet and poured water into the wash basin.

“I tried to call you but there was no way you could hear me, so I sent Sophia to get you. She ran right up as soon as I told her to go. It’s like she understood me.”

“I doubt she understands anything more than something is wrong with her mistress. But you did a good job, Sophia.”

The dog danced in a circle and licked Aunt Louellen’s hand. Then she whined again and lay with her head on the old woman’s lap.

Nellie wet a washcloth and wiped the blood off Aunt Louellen’s face. A bruise was forming over her eye with a tiny cut in the middle. It had stopped bleeding, so Nellie wiped it carefully and then cleaned the lower part of the old woman’s face. “Thank God it isn’t any worse than this. I thought I might see her brain under all that blood.

“She fought me, and fell and hit her head on the bed table. I’m sorry, Nellie. I was trying to help.”

“You did nothing wrong, I assure you. She has more wrong with her than a simple headache. She doesn’t have a fever. Was she delirious?”

“No, I don’t think so. It was like she couldn’t see where the floor was. Or maybe she couldn’t feel it. Either way, her leg gave out as soon as she tried to use it.”

“I’m going for Dr. Grey. Will you be okay here by yourself?”

Chloe nodded.

Nellie ran upstairs and dressed as fast as she could. Then she hurried through town to Dr. Grey’s house. He answered her first knock, already dressed with a cup of coffee in his hand.

“Your aunt took a turn for the worst?” At Nellie’s nod he reached behind the door for his bag and set his coffee cup on the hall table.

Nellie described what happened as they drove to the house. The doctor left the car and hurried up the walk. Chloe had the front door open before he got there and showed him to Aunt Louellen’s room.

Sophia dashed out of the open door and ran to Nellie. Nellie squatted down and scratched the little dog behind her ears. Sophie dropped to the ground and rolled onto her back for a belly rub. Nellie obliged, taking comfort in the simple antics of the dog.

She went inside through the kitchen door and found Chloe at the table nursing a cup of tea. The younger woman stared at Nellie with red rimmed eyes. “I fell asleep,” she confessed.

“Aunt Louellen was asleep. I thought we agreed the person on the night shift could sleep as long as Aunt Louellen was sleeping.”

“Yes, but she woke up and I didn’t hear her.”

“Chloe, we had a long day and you were tired. You didn’t do anything wrong. Something is going on here and none of us knows what it is. We’ll have to wait and see what Dr. Grey says. You’re fine.”

The kitchen door opened again and Emily entered, pale and drawn. “I barely slept. Is she okay? I saw Dr. Grey’s car.”

“He’s with her now. We won’t know until he comes out.”

“I’m doing laundry,” said Emily and disappeared into the pantry. She hauled the machine into the kitchen and started her first load.

Nellie spread butter on slices of bread that the three women gagged down around cups of strong tea. The wait went on for what felt like hours.

Finally, Dr. Grey emerged from the bedroom wearing a grim expression on his tired face.

"How long until Mr. Burke arrives?" he asked as he accepted the cup of tea Nellie handed him.

"I'm not sure. He didn't say when he left last night. I expect him any time, though it'll take them a while to drive up from Walton."

The doctor nodded and sank into a chair at the table. He wiped his face with his wrinkled hands. "Do you have another slice of bread? I didn't have a chance to eat before I left."

Nellie jumped to get it for him, thankful for something to do. They waited in silence while the doctor ate. Nellie helped Emily wring out the laundry. They were hanging it on the line when they saw Warren's car drive up their street.

"I believe she's had a stroke," said Dr. Grey as soon as Warren was in the kitchen. "I should have seen it last night, but I didn't. She had all the symptoms, confusion, headache, inability to use her limbs. Only time will tell how severe it is. I gave her another draught of the medicine but we're going to need to look into long-term treatment for her. Probably live-in nursing or placing her in a sanitarium. It will be up to you. I recommend you consult with her primary doctor to make the final decision."

"Dr. Greene is her primary doctor," said Warren.

"Good. A man I trust and respect. We can call him this morning and get his opinion."

Warren went with Dr. Grey to make the call while Nellie and Chloe slipped into the room to check on Aunt Louellen.

She was awake and somewhat lucid when Nellie tried to talk to her, but grew more and more agitated the longer they were there. Nellie felt her own frustration grow when Aunt Louellen shoved the water Nellie offered her away and a large portion of it slopped all over the bed.

"Who are you?" the old lady asked. She scrabbled at the coverlet and pulled it to her chest as if it offered some protection against Nellie.

"I'm Eleanor, Aunt Louellen. I've been living with you for the last few months."

"I don't know who you are," Aunt Louellen said. A tear slid down her cheek. "I don't know where I am."

"I'm here to help you," Nellie assured her. "You must be thirsty. Would you like a drink?"

She offered what remained in the glass and Aunt Louellen reluctantly took a drink. Once the first of the water touched her lips, she took the glass from Nellie and gulped the rest. Then she sank into the pillows and closed her eyes.

"Yes," she said after a moment, her words barely intelligible. "Yes, I remember. I remember who you are and where I am. Everything is so fuzzy. I can't keep my thoughts straight. When is Warren coming back from his trip?"

"He's back, Auntie. He'll be here in a minute."

Aunt Louellen's brow wrinkled in confusion. "I remember that now. Eleanor, I can't keep anything straight in my head." Terror covered her face and she grabbed for Nellie's hand.

Nellie held Aunt Louellen's hand and stroked her finger over the wrinkly skin on its back. She didn't know what to say or do to soothe this dear lady or to help her feel better. Several minutes passed before Aunt Louellen relaxed and went to sleep.

Nellie sat with her until she heard Warren and Dr. Grey return. Chloe had been cowering in the corner, fear and uncertainty covering her face. Nellie motioned her forward. "I need to find out what Daddy wants them to do. You sit here. Come get us if she needs anything."

Chloe, eyes wide, nodded. She dropped onto the chair beside the bed and gripped the seat with both hands.

Nellie felt for the girl. She remembered visiting the children's ward at the hospital in Walton. She'd felt the same emotions Chloe exhibited — terror and uncertainty. She rested her hand on Chloe's shoulder and squeezed. The girl forced a strained smile as she relaxed her grip on the chair.

"None of this is your fault, Chloe," Nellie whispered to assure her.

Chloe gave a stiff nod and stared straight ahead. Nellie squeezed her shoulder one more time before she went in search of the two men.

Warren and Dr. Grey were talking in the kitchen. Warren met Nellie's questioning gaze with a frown when she entered. He held up his hand and Dr. Grey stopped talking.

“Nellie needs to hear this. For Dr. Greene’s plan to work, we’ll need everyone’s help.”

“What does my father want us to do?”

“He trusts Dr. Grey’s diagnosis and wants us to bring Aunt Louellen back to Boston where hospitals will be better equipped to deal with her needs.”

“How can we do that?” Nellie sank onto a kitchen chair and leaned on the table. The thought of what her father was asking overwhelmed her. “She can’t even leave her bedroom right now.”

“I’ll get a nurse from the hospital at Walton,” said Dr. Grey. “I can be back by this afternoon and the nurse can spend the night. After what happened last night, we need someone here with more skill.”

Relief flooded Nellie. She’d been dreading the coming night. They had no idea what they were doing. A nurse could give them direction.

“Meanwhile,” Warren continued, “we’ll travel on the first train south tomorrow. Your father is going to make arrangements for an ambulance to meet us on that end. She can have proper care by tomorrow evening at the latest.”

“What chance of recovery does she have?” Nellie asked the question to which she most feared the answer. What if Aunt Louellen never recovered?

“We can’t say at this point. But it’s safe to assume her life will never be the same as it was. She’ll always need assistance. She’s old. She’s lived a full life. The best we can hope for is to make the rest of her days as comfortable as possible.”

Days? Not years? Nellie wanted to cry. She swallowed hard several times around the pain in her throat.

"It's my fault," she said. "I shouldn't have made her so mad at me." Her voice caught in a sob.

Warren pulled her into his arms. Dr. Grey patted her shoulder.

"It's not anyone's fault," said Dr. Grey. "No one knows why these things happen. She told you she'd had a headache all day. Numbers of people have reported their loved ones became irritable and had a change of demeanor before a stroke. She probably wasn't completely in control of herself and her response to you."

Dr. Grey's words made sense but they didn't make Nellie feel any better. She pulled away from Warren and forced a smile when he searched her face. They could talk more in private, but this wasn't the time.

"I'm going to Walton this morning for my usual rounds at the hospital. I'll check with Nurse Rogers about a nurse to travel with you to Boston. I'm sure we'll have everything arranged by this afternoon. You should see to the packing so you're ready to travel."

Nellie nodded and swiped at the tears on her cheeks. Warren's hands lingered on her shoulders while he searched her face. She managed a weak smile.

"I'm going to Walton, too," he said. "I'll make arrangements for the train and for transporting the trunks there tomorrow. Can you get someone to help you so you're ready?"

"Emily is already here and I'll see if Mrs. Stuart can come for a couple hours. I was planning to pay them to clean the house well once we leave. I don't want to leave a mess for my mama."

Warren drew her towards himself and kissed her forehead. "We'd better get started so everything is ready in time."

"I'll have Chloe start packing Auntie's clothes. Poor girl is beside herself. She needs something to do."

They each went their separate ways. By the time Dr. Grey brought a nurse that afternoon, they had the packing well in hand and had finished most of the cleaning. The trunks were stacked by the front door when they went to bed that night.

Nellie fell into bed that night, exhausted. Even her concerns about the following day couldn't keep her awake long.

Chapter Twenty-nine

Nellie sank into the cushioned chair in the train carriage and heaved a huge sigh of relief. Warren entered and sat next to her. She wished they had more privacy but Chloe and Nurse Painter were seated next to them, with Aunt Louellen tucked into the bed across from them, sound asleep. Peters was driving the car to Boston and had left as soon as it was light that morning.

They'd all said a teary goodbye at her parent's house. Mrs. Stuart and Emily had come over in time to see them off. Emily hugged all of them as if she'd never see them again. She'd paused when she came to Peters. That young man had lingered over the goodbye longer than Nellie thought appropriate, given how long they'd known each other. Nellie thought she saw him slip Emily a piece of paper, but she couldn't be sure. Now, as she thought over it, she decided not to worry. The distance between Boston and Hollis was far enough they wouldn't be able to get into any trouble. At least she hoped not, anyway.

The next challenge had been getting Aunt Louellen into the car and comfortable. Every movement caused her pain and even sitting in the car had been uncomfortable. She couldn't remember Nellie or Chloe and fought the nurse when she tried to dress and feed her. Warren had been the only one able to get her to do anything. He gently reminded her who Nellie was and that she was sick and needed the nurse's help. Aunt Louellen pouted for a moment. Then they could see her memory gradually return like it had the day before. She cooperated with the nurse and tried to eat the food they gave her.

But the travel was too much. They'd given up riding in Dr. Grey's car. Nellie had ridden in the cab of the lory carrying their luggage and Warren had ridden in the back. Aunt Louellen lay back as best she could in the doctor's car, with blankets and cushions tucked around her. They'd driven so slowly, Nellie feared they'd miss the train.

Yet, here they were, sitting in their carriage with the Maine countryside flying by the window.

Warren slid his hand into Nellie's and squeezed her fingers. She smiled up at him. She longed to lean into his chest and close her eyes. The clatter of the tracks made private conversation difficult.

Then Nellie heard Warren's voice in her ear. "I have some surprises for you back in Boston. Things I brought with me from all over Europe. I almost brought them to Hollis, but now I'm glad I didn't. We have something to look forward to in Boston."

If Chloe or Nurse Painter knew he was talking, they gave no indication. Pleasure spread through Nellie. "What kind of surprises?"

Warren's eyes sparkled. "If I told you, they wouldn't be surprises anymore, would they?"

Nellie tried to glare at him, but she couldn't hide her smile. "Did you get Aunt Louellen her perfume?

She was hoping for it. Though now I'm not sure she'll even remember she asked."

"I did. It's with the other things in Boston. Maybe it will be what she needs to perk up."

"Dr. Grey said she may never perk up." The ever-present sadness of the last several days descended on Nellie again.

"Then we'll help her enjoy whatever time she has left."

"You don't need me any more. She'll need a nurse from now on."

"She'll always need you, Nellie. You're the best thing that happened to her in years. You're the best thing that ever happened to me. I need you, even if she doesn't."

Nellie lifted her eyes to Warren's. His were so close, so full of everything he couldn't say with other people around.

"Nellie, I need you with me for the rest of my life. Nellie..."

Nellie placed her finger over his lips to stop anything else he wanted to say. He kissed it and she dropped her hand back to her lap, hoping the other two women hadn't seen anything.

"You're right," he whispered. "This isn't the time or place. You deserve something so much better."

The nurse was reading a book in her lap. Chloe had already fallen asleep. Nellie rested her head on the seat back. The clack of the wheels on the tracks had a hypnotic effect, her eyes slid shut despite her efforts to stay awake.

Nellie woke when they arrived in Portland. This time, they had to change trains. It took all four of them to get Aunt Louellen and their luggage situated. Once the train was moving again, they pulled out the lunch Mrs. Stuart had sent with them. The nurse helped Aunt Louellen eat and drink and Nellie took care of Sophia. Aunt Louellen fell asleep again.

This stretch of track felt endless. They couldn't smell the ocean any more and wouldn't for several hours as the track moved inland. The carriage got warmer as they left the cooler weather behind. Added to everything was the uncertainty they all felt about the situation.

Hours later, Dr. Greene met them at the station with an ambulance as promised. He escorted Aunt Louellen to the hospital while Warren, Nellie, and Chloe dealt with the trunks and made arrangements for Nurse Painter's return to Walton.

They got everything to Aunt Louellen's house. Reynolds had opened the house and the cleaning lady had come to put everything back in order. Cook had prepared them a light supper. They ate wearily. Chloe disappeared into Aunt Louellen's room to unpack before she went home for the night.

Nellie found Warren in his study. He was on the phone so she left and returned a few minutes later. He sat in his favorite chair, staring into the empty fireplace. Nellie watched from the doorway. She'd missed coming into the room and finding him like that. Pleasure filled her as he looked up and smiled, happy to see her.

"Come. Sit," he said.

Nellie took her normal seat.

"I phoned Aunt Louellen's solicitor. He's concerned about her finances. It appears they are more depleted than I thought. There's enough for us to make her comfortable here at home with a nurse for the indefinite future, but not enough to pay for a sanatarium."

Nellie frowned. She hadn't realized finances were an issue. "Should we have been more careful the last few months?"

"What?" Warren frowned as well. Then he understood. "No. Please don't worry about anything. I was assessing the situation if her care became long term. No, you've done nothing except give my aunt the best of your care and attention. The last few months have been the the most enjoyable she's had in years. She told me that yesterday."

"She was barely coherent yesterday."

"When I sat with her, she seemed to remember most of what she'd forgotten. The doctor said her memory would fade in and out. She said she wished her life didn't have to be over."

"It doesn't have to be over."

"She's old, Nellie. She won't recover from this no matter how much we want her to."

"Then we'll make the months or years she has left as good as we can."

"Nellie, my darling Nellie. I love how much you love her." Warren caught Nellie's hand and lifted it to his lips. He turned it over and kissed her palm, then her wrist.

Nellie thrilled at his touch, until her better judgement took over and she pulled her arm away. "I came to talk to you about that."

"How much you love my aunt?" asked Warren, a twinkle in his eye.

"No, how much..." Nellie hesitated. "I came to talk about the fact that we can't stay here alone in the same house. It wouldn't be proper."

"I've been thinking about it, too," said Warren, suddenly serious. "I'll get a hotel for a couple nights. Once Aunt Louellen is back with her nurse, I can stay here again."

Nellie took a deep breath. She knew he might not like her idea, but it was the only logical option. "It would be silly for you to spend money on a hotel. I can stay at my aunt's and uncle's house again. They still have a room I can use. My parent's are living in a small apartment until they can find something more permanent. They don't have room for me. But my aunt and uncle will let me stay there as long as needed."

"How will you get there?"

"I'll have to get a cab. We can phone them to let them know I'm coming, but my father told me he'd informed them of the situation and they said they would help however they could. This is a good way for them to help."

Warren returned his eyes to the fireplace, a sign he was thinking.

"I've been away from you so much the last few months. I was looking forward to having you and Aunt Louellen here, to going back to how things were before I left."

"Things will never go back to how they were before you left." Nellie gently took his hand in both of hers. He covered her smaller hands with his, encasing them completely. “I’m not going anywhere. I’ll see you at the hospital and you can call at my aunt’s and uncle’s whenever you want.”

“I can take you to dinner and the theater, just the two of us.”

“We’ll have to be properly chaperoned, of course.”

“Of course.”

Warren stroked her hands. When his eyes met hers and he spoke again, his voice was deep, earnest. “Nellie, will you marry me?”

His question shocked Nellie. She hadn’t expected it.

He went on. “I’d planned to do something fancy and special. But now, all I want is to have this settled, to go to bed tonight knowing at least this one thing is certain.”

Nellie didn’t know what to say. She loved him and could see his love for her. Yet the old, familiar fear gripped her heart. What if this turned out like before?

“I’ve already spoken to your father about it. I talked with him before I even came up to Hollis to see you. He’s given his permission. He said he wasn’t surprised.”

Nellie still hesitated. She wanted to say ‘yes’. She wanted to be married to Warren more than anything in the world.

As if Warren could see her fear, he whispered, “Wherever you are is home for me.”

“Yes,” Nellie breathed. “Yes, I’ll marry you.”

Warren stood and caught Nellie in his arms, pulling her up with him. He crushed her against himself. Nellie clung to him.

“My darling, my darling,” he breathed against her hair.

The sound of someone clearing their throat in the open doorway made Nellie jump, but not Warren. He slid his arms to her waist. They faced Reynolds who wore a grim expression. Warren didn't seem to care. He was beaming.

"Reynolds! Miss Greene agreed to marry me."

"That's nice, sir. What will her parents say?"

Warren gazed down at Nellie, eyes full of love. "I wouldn't have asked if they hadn't given permission, Reynolds."

Reynolds sighed. "Will I be needing to spend the night here, sir?"

Warren laughed, a loud, joyful sound that should have been contagious. Nellie couldn't stop the smile that had spread across her face. But Reynolds continued to look grim.

"I appreciate your concern, but Miss Greene will be moving to her aunt's and uncle's house until Aunt Louellen comes home. I'll be calling her a cab and escorting her there shortly."

Reynolds gave one short nod and turned to leave, but Nellie could see the relief wash over his face. Everything must be done properly under Reynolds' watchful eye.

Warren caught Nellie's chin and brought her gaze up to his. Then he kissed her. "I've waited so long for you," he whispered against her lips.

Nellie had to agree.

Chapter Thirty

Nine months later

Nellie hesitated at the bottom of the gang plank, until Warren gave her a little push to get her going. "I've never been on an ocean liner before," she said.

"Then you are in for a real treat. Especially if we get into a storm. Yessiree. Days and days of rocking and nausea. As if you haven't had enough of that already."

Nellie stopped and Warren bumped into her. "This is a bad idea."

He laughed in her ear. "It's not that bad, and you're going to have a good time. I promise. I will personally see to your enjoyment on this trip."

Nellie flushed a deep red at his words.

Warren bumped her again. "We're holding up the line."

Once they'd found their cabin and their belongings were stowed, Nellie tried to relax and enjoy herself. They strolled around the deck, watching the crew make last-minute preparations as late comers hurriedly embarked.

"We shouldn't have left her like we did," said Nellie. "You know how she gets when we change things."

"Aunt Louellen wanted us to come. She said it several times. You heard her."

"Yes, but she needs us. She won't always be around."

"Travel is only going to get harder over the next few months, impossible a few months after that. At least until our little one is older," said Warren. He rested his hand on Nellie's still flat belly.

"Warren!" Nellie breathed in horror, but she couldn't hide the pleased expression that followed as she turned away.

"We've been married for five months and haven't had a honeymoon. Aunt Louellen knows we haven't. Now the weather is nice again, we have no reason not to travel." Warren rested a hand on the rail on either side of Nellie, his chest against her back. "She loves the nurse. She has Chloe. They all get on fine. Try not to worry."

Nellie sighed with contentment and leaned against Warren. She didn't care if anyone saw.

"You'll probably feel better once we're underway," Warren assured her, his lips next to her ear.

"I'm sure you're right," she said. "I'm nervous because I've never traveled anywhere like this before."

"I know." Warren sounded like a schoolboy, eager, excited. "I can hardly wait to show you everything. I'm sure we'll find new things to discover together. Don't worry about Aunt Louellen. She wants to hear about your first trip. She'd have come if she could. My suspicion is she'll hang around to hear all about it when we get back."

Nellie scanned first one way on the deck, then the other. They were alone. She turned to face Warren and wrapped her arms around his neck. "Thank you," she breathed against his lips. Then she kissed him.

He groaned and pulled her closer. "I love it when you do that," he whispered back. His hand cradled her head as he deepened the kiss.

"Do what?" Nellie asked when he stopped kissing her, though she already knew.

"When you pretend to be coy, but then surprise me with something bold like," he gasped and stage whispered, "kissing me on the deck when people could be watching."

"We aren't in the privacy of our own home anymore."

"Our home hasn't ever been private and yet we've managed. You know why?"

"Why?" Nellie asked, though she knew the answer to this as well. Her eyes twinkled at him in anticipation.

"Because wherever we are is home. This ship, Aunt Louellen's house, anywhere, as long as we're together. I choose you, Eleanor Burke."

The foghorn sounded and the liner lurched under their feet as the tugboats pushed it away from the dock. Nellie gasped and gripped the rail, while holding Warren's arm with the other hand. His strong hand supported her back and she leaned into him. Together, they watched Boston Harbor fade into the distance as the horizon stretched in front of them, full of the promise of wonderful things to come.

Author's Note

Nellie was quite the antagonist in Promising Meg. For years, I was happy she got what she had coming to her. Then, one day, I began to feel sorry for her.

I began to wonder what her story would be. How would she fall in love? Who would that man be? What could happen to her to shape her into the kind of woman a man would want to spend the rest of his life with? And so, Nellie's story began to form. I envisioned her story and began to see the potential for an entire series of stories about strong women through the beginning of the 20th century.

I hope you enjoy watching Nellie change and grow like I did while I wrote the book.

Acknowledgements

Thank you to my beta readers, Rachel Miller, Suzy Oakley, Kris Loomis, and Judy Sutton. Your suggestions were invaluable and I took every one of them to heart.

Thank you to every one of my ARC readers. You guys are a huge help getting this book out there, into the wild, where people can read and enjoy it.

Thank you James, for putting up with my endless discussions about romance novels, my endless writing projects, and for giving your ideas when I ask. I suppose there is some quid pro quo going on here. I can now carry on an informed discussion about comic book superheroes having never read a comic myself, solely from listening to you talk about them. I love you! <3

Thank you, Indestructible Author accountability group. You guys are a constant motivation and help.

Thanks to the Create If group and our fearless leader, Kirsten. You all inspire me to try things I wouldn't otherwise attempt.

Finally, I'm so thankful to God for making a way for selfish, arrogant individuals like Nellie and me, to be transformed into the image of His Son.

Look for other books by Anna Huckabee on her Amazon Author page including her Lincoln Square series.

Follow Anna on her blog: A Huckabee Author and sign up for her email update to stay apprised of any future releases.

Made in the USA
Middletown, DE
25 November 2024